Life of a Drum

'Beautifully crafted . . . a deceptively quiet novel of considerable ambition'

Sunday Tribune

'A triumph of sensibility over sense'

Observer

'This book has a satisfying philosophical resonance which lifts it above the minutely observed details of the characters' behaviour'

She

'Hypnotic to read, Gébler manages to give the novel page-turning tension'

Irish Times

Also by Carlo Gébler:

THE ELEVENTH SUMMER
AUGUST IN JULY
WORK AND PLAY
DRIVING THROUGH CUBA
MALACHY AND HIS FAMILY
THE GLASS CURTAIN

For children:

THE TV GENIE
THE WITCH THAT WASN'T

Life of a Drum

CARLO GÉBLER

An *Abacus* Book

First published in Great Britain in 1991 by Hamish Hamilton
This edition published in 1992 by Abacus

A CIP catalogue record for this book
is available from the British Library.

ISBN 0 349 10218 X

Printed and bound in Great Britain by
Cox & Wyman Ltd, Reading, Berkshire

Abacus
A Division of
Little, Brown and Company (UK) Limited
165 Great Dover Street
London SE1 4YA

For
Helen Quinn
and
Marian Richardson

Prologue

How do you explain these things?

You could say, 'I need the money. I came home and went to bed with him.'

You could say, 'The flesh is weak. I came home and went to bed with him.'

You could say, 'I take comfort wherever I can. I came home and went to bed with him.'

That's all fine and dandy as far as it goes, but it's not the truth.

I went home with him, drunk. I undressed, drunk. I went to bed with him, drunk.

Now that's a truth.

I don't know what you would call what happened next. He lifted his great heavy shape on to me and we moved together but the earth did not move.

We are neither of us sexual athletes. We are neither of us getting any younger. We're inept. We're hopeless. Yet we held each other as if this was the very last time. We were even tender.

That's another truth.

Life's a series of blows. What is it Rudi used to say? 'What is born a drum is beaten till death.'

Now, that's a truth.

My story on a postcard;
Once upon a time it was March and I was about to go to Brighton with my husband. He was what they call a petty crook. He wasn't anything of the sort to me but that's how he would be described by some. But now he is dead and gone and I am with Johnnie, the man I met the day Rudi died.

And now it is the end of summer and I am in a bedroom in Primrose Hill. Another man I loved is downstairs. He is the third man in all this. He is talking to my new lover. They own this house together.

I was lying here with Johnnie after our love-making when we heard, first the taxi pulling up outside and then the front door opening and banging shut as Claus came in.

'I'm going down to talk to him,' announced Johnnie, and he got up, pulled on a dressing-gown to cover his square, heavy body and went out.

And since he left I have been lying here and thinking, How did it happen?

SPRING

One

1

'We mightn't be able to let you have the time off work, after all,' Mr Sammi joked that lunchtime.

We were in the so-called office, a small, airless box at the back of the Praed Street premises. It's from here that Mr Sammi controls his chain of dry-cleaners.

I looked up from the ledger with its yellow pages and blue feint lines. I was getting the accounts ready before my fortnight off. I'm both the clerk and his secretary.

My cheeks went red. Mr Sammi saw and was suddenly sorry for what he'd said. He didn't know how to get himself out of the mess and I didn't see what I could say either that would help, so I bent over my ledger and started adding up a column of figures.

Then, in the afternoon, he told me to go home early on account of it being the start of my holiday. He can be nice sometimes, like that.

'Goodbye,' he said.

'Goodbye.'

I was vaguely anxious something was going to happen – I didn't know what, but something – and Mr Sammi was going to smile and say, 'Hang on, Mrs J. We can't let you go, after all.' This is his idea of humour

7

and, while most of the time I play along with it, I wasn't in the mood that afternoon. So I walked smartly out of the premises and into the street.

Not far from my bus stop on Praed Street there were a couple of gypsy women patrolling the pavements. Heavy women with thick arms and hanging jowls.

I hate the way they bar your path and then say, 'Piece of heather, dearie? Bring you luck!' in a voice which is meant to sound friendly but we all know is really a threat. You find this out when you say 'No' and they curse you.

I'm a coward of course and I always say 'Yes'. So rather than have them accost me and then wait at the bus stop holding a piece of heather, resenting them for bullying me and myself for caving in and paying them a pound or whatever they were going to charge, I decided to take the tube instead. I nipped over the road and slipped into the station.

Inside Paddington it was dark on account of the layers of dirt lying on the glass roof. There were men hauling mail bags out of a Post Office van and throwing them on to a trolley, while somewhere overhead pigeons were cooing and fluttering their wings.

To get to the Metropolitan Line you have to walk down the whole length of the station. There was a blue-and-white train stationed beside the platform which I walked along. I was very taken by the notices stuck up in the windows that read 'Cornish Riviera'. Definition signs always raise my spirits, on account, I suppose, of years working abroad.

Then I noticed the strong smell of tea – that stewed tea smell which always seems to hang around railway stations – and I thought to myself, lovely. I remembered that smell from when I was a child.

Suddenly, I felt happy. Not the over-the-moon kind of happy but the quiet, more contented variety. The sort the old tell you about when you're young and you find hard to believe – I did, anyway – and then later, as you get older, you discover for yourself.

The underground station where I caught my train is actually overground. You look down from the platform on to the silver tracks that run into Paddington.

After I'd waited a few minutes, my train appeared. I got on and found a seat. There was an empty bottle on the floor and it rolled around making a terrible racket. It was obviously irritating evrybody but nobody did anything. We never do act in these situations, do we? It's as if we're paralysed.

Then after a while I thought, Oh sod it! and the next time the bottle clattered by I trapped it with my foot.

Nobody reacted except for the man sitting opposite. He put his head out from behind his paper, nodded at me and then went back to his reading.

This gave me the licence to look at his paper, I decided. On the page in front of me there was an article about the French Revolution. The two-hundredth anniversary was coming up and all the papers were full of it.

The writer's gist – I didn't have time to take it all in – was that the French got rid of their king and cut off his head, only to find, twenty years later, that they had a new king in the person of Napoleon. We think we can change our systems and structures, said the writer with a flourish, but we can't.

But do we always have to revert, I wondered. Is there

never, ever, any escape?

In the middle of the page there was a picture of one of those carts carrying a couple through the crowds to the guillotine. 'Tumbril on its way to the scaffold', the caption read.

That was all I had time for because then I was at Royal Oak. I got out and climbed up the stairs to the street. As I walked down Porchester Road, I started thinking about the picture. Did the people in the French crowds actually look the victims in the eye, I wondered. Or just jeer while pretending not to see the terrified expressions on their faces? Rudi, who saw people in a worse light than I did, would probably have said the mob did look and, worse, that they did enjoy what they saw. When he got home, I decided, I was going to ask him.

I don't know and I can't prove it but I don't think we're all bad. All right, the human race has done some terrible things, but I can't believe all of us are rotten, right to the core.

We do love each other, or we try to love each other, sometimes. I loved Rudi in my own way, not that I showed him enough of that. I could and should have shown him more, but it's too late now to do anything about that. Next time I'll do better, if there is a next time.

Yes, the French got a king back with Napoleon and the writer was right; we do revert to type. But aren't we also able to learn from experience? I have. I am going to be better. I want to be. I must be. And I will be responsible for what I do.

On the other hand, there's no end to our ability to muck things up, is there? And has it not happened again? Is this a muck-up? I don't know. I can't answer the question, any more than I can decide whether the drum has any chance of escaping, or changing its circumstances.

You can work yourself into a frazzle thinking about these things and never settle the matter. All I know is that from here on in, I'm not going to let myself be tossed about like a cork on the sea.

I had several letters of Mr Sammi's to post. At the corner I turned into Westbourne Grove and walked along to the pillar-box. As I put each letter through the slot, I listened for the sound of it dropping into the wire cage inside. It's something I always do. Extra insurance that a letter is on its way. It may be a sign of weakness but I've long since given up struggling against it.

Then I turned round and went back to Bishop's Bridge Road and, a hundred yards further along, came to Westbourne Mansions. This is home.

It's a mansion block, a big, square, red-brick affair, with cream-coloured windows. The way into the building is through a huge arch at the front with two enormous wooden gates set into it. The gates are only opened from time to time – when, for instance, the lorry has to come in and suck out the sewage from the tank under the courtyard. Otherwise, they are kept shut, and the actual way in and out is through a little door set into the gate on the left. I've only ever seen the same arrangement in a prison.

I turned the brass door handle to open the small door and stepped over the door-sill. Inside I found myself in a short dark tunnel that runs under the front of the block, and at the far end I came out into the oblong courtyard. The walls were red brick again; the railings along the landings rising on all sides were yellow; and the bells in the middle of the front doors of each of the flats were black, like the pupil of an eye.

The very first flat which you come to belongs to the caretaker, and her dog immediately started up behind the net curtains. It's a poodle, with wet marks under his eyes. He usually clings desperately to my legs when I have to call on her and tries to mate.

Rudi's trick, when he passed sometimes, was to slow down and drag his feet on the floor. This used to whip poor old Tommy inside into such a frenzy, you'd hear him in the Smalls' living-room leaping from sofa to armchair and back again, barking his little head off, and Reg or Mrs Small shouting at him, 'Oi, Tommy, stop that, will you!' or something like that.

I could see why Rudi did it but I didn't like it. Why torment the animal, I used to say to him. It was the Smalls who were really at fault for keeping him locked up for so long that he had become certifiable.

'Oh yes, what a nation of animal-lovers you are!' Rudi used to say to me sarcastically when I said this. 'All your old people leave their money to the dogs' homes, while your poor go hungry. This, I suppose, is what you will do.'

Rudi came from a harder world than we do and he didn't see life as I did.

At the back of the courtyard I came to my stair-well and started climbing. The treads are stone with silvery flecks which flicker. Tommy was still yapping.

I reached the landing on the first floor. It was Friday and this is the day Mrs Small does her so-called cleaning of the common parts. There were cloudy pools of disinfectant lying here and there in the hollows and dips in the floor.

She had opened one of the windows to air the place and, as the sash-cord was broken, she had wedged a piece of broomstick under it.

I looked down on to the courtyard with its red asphalt floor, Mrs Small's flat on the corner with its brass plaque which read 'Caretaker', and the wooden gates with the small door inset like the way into a prison. Then I pulled the broomstick away and lowered the window, after which I couldn't see any more because the glass in the pane is frosted.

The next moment the dog stopped. I started climbing the stairs again. I remembered how exited I had felt that morning and I wondered where the feeling had gone. It wasn't that I was sad; it was just that I wasn't 'up' like I had been.

You're going on a holiday, I reminded myself. You're going to Brighton.

I found my key and unlocked the front door. I felt excited again and I realized I'd got the feeling back.

I remembered my new suit which I had bought for the occasion and that it was hanging in the wardrobe. It was still in the polythene from the dry-cleaners and for a moment I imagined that dry-cleaning smell it would have when I unwrapped it. I'd got it done for free at work, one of our few perks.

I'd not tried the suit on, I remembered, since getting it home. I went cheerfully into my flat and closed the door.

2

When I was twenty, I left my home in Sussex and came up to London. For the first few months I stayed with a friend from school called Emma Griff-Douglas. Her father had bought her a flat in Barons Court to live in while she was at London University.

Every morning, when I set off for work, Emma would be lying in the bath, stretched out in the hot water, and from the hall as I called goodbye, I would see her pale form reflected in the steamed-up mirror over the sink.

This is one of a series of memories which, when I run them together, form a picture of my whole life.

Before I came up, I had done a secretarial and book-keeping course at a college in Brighton. My ambitions were to work and to travel.

After some months of temporary jobs in the City, none of them very interesting, it was arranged for me to see a Mr Anstruther. I was told that he would be able to give me the kind of job I was looking for.

The arrangement was made through Shirley. She was Emma Griff-Douglas's best friend's sister's oldest friend, or something. I forget the exact connection. This

14

was all some years ago.

In order to talk to me about the coming interview, Shirley invited me to tea. We met in a café in Marylebone High Street which smelt of confectioner's sugar and coffee. The customers were women who wore powder and perfume and kept their hats on while they ate.

I ordered an éclair and a coffee with cream. Shirley only drank black tea and smoked Disque Bleu. I knew she had once been a dancer and reckoned she was in her early fifties.

I was not going through a very happy time. I had a boyfriend who worked for Shell and who was going out to Africa. I wanted to tell Shirley how hurt I felt and that I was going to miss him. I imagined she was experienced and wise, and would have been able to help me get it all in perspective, and I wished I'd known her better and could have confided in her.

I finished the éclair and she ordered me a piece of cheesecake, telling me it was the best in London, and while I ate it she told me, enthusiastically, about the pleasures of 'abroad'.

The appointment with Mr Anstruther was on one of the last days of December, after Christmas and before the New Year. I had been staying in Sussex with my mother, and on the day of the interview I caught the train up to town.

I was anxious. No, I was more than anxious, I was in a state. For the whole week I'd been home with my mum, I had been tortured by the idea of the interview which was getting closer and closer. I'd kept having these awful daydreams in which, in answer to the simplest questions, I had given the most awful replies. It was as if I had been dreaming up the worst way an interview could go.

Now, on the train, invented conversations of this kind swirled again inside my head. In the background was the clatter of the wheels which I could hear below me on the tracks, and the swaying of the tinsel which some revellers returning from a Christmas party had hung in great loops from the luggage rack on the other side of the carriage.

It now sounds so unlikely but I got myself into such a state on the journey that I started a head-cold. I went hot and cold, my throat started to ache and my nose began to drip.

When I reached Waterloo, I wanted to ring Mr Anstruther's office and cancel. Then I reasoned with myself that all I would be achieving would be a postponement. I would still have to go through all this at some point in the future.

It was the middle of the afternoon when I found myself in Queen's Gate.

The trees along the pavement were bare and dripping. A mist was forming and it was beginning to get dark. A few people appeared out of the gloom, swathed in hats and coats, and then disappeared again as quickly as they had come.

I was feverish and I had wiped my nose so often that the skin underneath was red. In one hand I had an A–Z and in the other a piece of paper with Mr Anstruther's address.

I believed that the mews where Mr Anstruther had his office was near the park. But when I got there I found that his mews, which had almost the same name as the one I had gone to, was in fact at the other end of Queen's Gate from where I was – and it is a very long street.

When I realized my mistake, I was seized by a blind sense of panic. If I didn't hurry, I was going to be late. If I was late, then Mr Anstruther wouldn't see me. If he didn't see me, then I wouldn't get the job. If I didn't get the job, then what was I going to do? And how was I going to explain to Shirley and everyone along the chain why I was late for the interview?

I started running, not very efficiently or comfortably in the shoes I was wearing, and within seconds I felt beads of sweat springing up on my forehead and the back of my neck.

At the Cromwell Road I had to stop to wait for the traffic. My glowing face froze, while underneath my woollen coat, my wet blouse went cold and stuck to my skin.

I got across and hurried on. Where my fingers touched the *A–Z*, the paper was wet and swollen. Big white houses with paint peeling from their stucco towered above me and Queen's Gate seemed to stretch into the distance for ever. My legs felt like jelly. The sweat ran down my forehead, got into my eyes and stung them.

I had only one thought: I must get to my appointment. . . . Get it over . . .

Mr Anstruther's mews office, when I found it, was a small brick house painted blue with a plaque which read,

Prospero Import–Export Company
Teheran Beirut Riyadh

I pressed the bell. A few moments later a youngish woman opened the door, looked at me and said, 'What happened to you?'

'I've come for an appointment with Mr Anstruther,' I panted, 'I'm Catherine Baring. I'm not too late, I hope.'

'No, you're not late,' she said, 'but Mr Anstruther is. He's going to be late for his own funeral. He's not back from lunch yet.'

I followed her up the steep stairs to a room where the walls were covered with metallic bamboo wallpaper, and where Christmas cards hung from the fireplace on a piece of green twine.

She fetched me a green paper towel. I wiped my face and looked at the great wet stain I had made in the middle. It reminded me of the shape of a brain from one of my biology books at school.

I thought about my panic and my running and asked myself, What did I have to show for it all? A wet patch on a paper towel.

When Mr Anstruther arrived I was feeling sleepy but I rallied quickly and we shook hands. He had a strange smell about him, like steak-and-kidney pudding.

He was a big man, in his fifties, in a coat with a fur-trimmed collar. He wore his grey hair long, to the shoulder, which rather shocked me. The mental picture I had formed in advance of Mr Anstruther did not run to him looking like Wild Bill Hickok.

He brought me into his office. The light-bulb in the overhead light was gone and a replacement couldn't be found. I was snuffling and he lit a cigar. There were potted plants with dusty leaves and a reproduction medieval globe. The Christmas tree in the corner had shed most of its needles, and the solitary present which lay underneath on the floor was half-buried by them.

Mr Anstruther asked a few questions. Yes, I could type, I said, eighty words a minute, and I showed him the certificate. Yes, I could do shorthand, I said, and I showed him another certificate. And yes, I had business French, I said, and showed him a third. I had some book-keeping, I added. I wanted to show Mr Anstruther the next piece of paper I'd brought along, but he declined.

He led me to a room downstairs. It appeared to have once been the garage and was piled with tea-chests. There was a man behind a desk, completely surrounded by them.

'Ron . . . Catherine . . .' said Mr Anstruther briefly, waving his hand between the two of us, and then he glided from the room, leaving us alone.

Ron had short hair and wore a St Christopher medal which hung down the outside of his turtle-neck sweater.

'Okey-dokey,' said Ron, 'I'm going to put you through a few simple tests. Nothing gruesome.'

He sat me down in front of a battered Imperial typewriter and put an open book beside me. It was a collection of Noël Coward songs and the one on the page was 'Mad Dogs and Englishmen Go Out in the Midday Sun'.

I blew my nose and typed it out. He looked over what I'd done. I apologized for having a cold and explained I wasn't at my best. He dictated a letter and then gave me the first chapter of Genesis to type up.

I went back to wait in the room with the metallic bamboo wallpaper. The woman who'd opened the door gave me her *Daily Mail* to read.

In the office. I could hear Ron and Mr Anstruther talking but I couldn't make out what they were saying.

A few minutes later Ron came out and the secretary led me into Mr Anstruther's office. A light-bulb had been found, a very bright and powerful light-bulb, and the place was lit up like a film set.

Mr Anstruther stood up from behind his desk and shook my hand. In this way I gathered I had been a success. I would do some work with Ron, he told me, and in a week's time I would fly out to Teheran, to join Mr Anstruther's Iranian office.

In Barons Court that evening, Emma and I opened a bottle of wine to celebrate. I telephoned my mother.

'Is it a long way away?' she asked.

'It's beyond Turkey,' I said. I had had a look at a map – in Anstruther's office in fact, the secretary had shown it to me.

'I shall have to go to the library and look it up,' she said.

She didn't say 'Well done', or 'I'm so pleased for you', or anything like that because it's not her style. I knew in advance she wasn't going to congratulate me and yet I was still disappointed that she didn't. No matter how accustomed to someone you are, you can't ever stop yourself hoping they might change, can you?

Shirley appeared then and we started an excited conversation about what injections I was going to need for Teheran. I found myself forgetting about my mum.

20

We all talked at once.

'What about Mr Anstruther?' Shirley asked suddenly. 'Did he pounce?'

'No,' I said, 'Nothing like that happened. Is he like that?'

'Absolutely,' she said emphatically.

'He probably didn't try it on because of my nose,' I said, and we all laughed and laughed.

3

Mr Anstruther's Teheran office was in a flat in a high-rise apartment block. It was near the Charahei-Pahlavi, the Pahlavi Crossroads. This was a middle-class part of the city.

Six of us worked here. There were Pam and Sarah and Zeeta – all professional women in their twenties; a young boy called Aziz who ran errands in between reading comics; and Ron.

'What was Anstruther like at the interview?' asked Pam, the morning I arrived.

She was a small woman with blonde wavy hair who came from Yorkshire. One of the radiators had started leaking and we were laying Pyrex dishes underneath to catch the brown drips.

'He was fine,' I said. 'We talked a bit, I typed up some things, I got the job. That was all there was to it.'

We went and sat down on the long leather sofa in the office sitting-room. All the windows along one wall were open; above us stretched a blue winter's sky, while below lay the city, its streets filled with donkey-carts and porters with loads on their backs, battered lorries and crowded buses, rickety black bicycles and

Mercedes cars with tinted windows, all rushing against each other. On the ground there was an incredible din of car horns and hoarse shouting, but twenty-one floors above one could hear hardly anything.

'When I was on leave once,' said Pam, 'he invited me to come on a picnic, and after we'd finished eating he said, "Do you fancy a post-prandial fuck?" I didn't know what "prandial" meant, so I had to say, "No!"'

'Well, I don't know what it means either,' I said, and after she told me we laughed together.

There were curtains on the windows and, as the breeze blew, they billowed towards us, catching the flakes of rust shed by the metal window-frames and sweeping them along the floor.

The movement was faintly mesmerizing, like the sea. We watched it for a few moments and then Pam said, 'The place may be falling apart, but Teheran beats the Yorkshire Dales and a Sunday trip to Scarborough, any day.'

At lunchtime they sent Aziz out. He returned with cardboard boxes which were hot from the food inside, and the office was filled with the smell of spices. He laid everything out on the round, copper table in the sitting-room. There was lamb; a *khoresh* stew made with cauliflower; a salad of thin lettuce strips and another with kidney beans; pickles made from garlic, tamarind and aubergine; yoghurt and cucumber; and cans of Coca Cola with beads of cold water running down the sides.

Ron produced a bottle of arak. I drank several cloudy glasses and felt tipsy. I was toasted and welcomed by the others.

We finished half-way through the afternoon and it was time to go back to work. My place was immediately inside the front door. I had a telex machine, a small telephone switchboard, and a vast electric typewriter which hummed. I had to retype my first letter twice before I got it right.

After a few days I moved from the hotel where I was staying into Sarah's flat. She was a tall woman with teeth which sloped inwards. She rolled her own cigarettes with a silver Rizla rolling-machine which a boyfriend had given her. The inscription was in English and Cantonese. The boyfriend was a Hong Kong businessman and married. In the end he had stuck with his wife and Sarah had come to Teheran, to Prospero Import–Export.

The third woman in the office was Zeeta. She was from Durban, South Africa, a Eurasian. She was plump and her hair was long and black. She had an Armenian boyfriend who owned a restaurant. Every week she went to a bathhouse to be shaved. I went with her once. After doing her arms and legs, the attendant shaved her between her legs. It was a strange sight; Zeeta, naked on the slab and smooth as a shell.

With the women from the office, I started going to nightclubs and discothèques. The Ghsra Ea Yakh or Castle of Ice at the ice rink, Zhivago's, and the Cabaret Moulin Rouge. Many of the others were simply called 'Disco'. Yet no matter what the name, they were all the same: dim lights, small dance floors and large bars. I learnt to smoke and got a taste for whisky sours.

In the bars I made acquaintances; Europeans and Americans who'd come out to work in the oil industry, and any number of rich, middle-class Iranians. They were generous, arrogant, and there wasn't one who didn't nurse a sly grudge against the Shah.

I had many boyfriends, but Parvis was the nicest. He was not a businessman like the others, but a student at the university, studying languages. He approached me first because he wanted to practise his English, and then one thing led to another. I used to buy books for him from other Europeans and, after we had made love, we used to lie in bed and work our way through them together. Two of the books, I remember, were *Animal Farm* and *The Catcher in the Rye.*

Parvis had dark skin and long black eyelashes and he wore a small medallion round his neck with some words from the Koran on it. He taught them to me once but now I have forgotten them. He was the first person I would say that I loved.

After a year, he disappeared. It was rumoured he was in some sort of trouble with the government. I went round to see his parents. His mother wept and wrung a handkerchief in her hands while his father repeated, 'Bad, bad,' over and over again.

A year or so later I discovered he had died in prison of tuberculosis. Not knowing what has happened to someone is unbearable but knowing can be no great shakes either. Now I knew he had been in prison, I could be certain he had been beaten, or worse.

Something was festering in Iran and we could all smell it. Yet we all believed that if we just waited long enough, it would go away. We were wrong. The Shah fell and Mr Anstruther closed his office on the twenty-first floor and moved us to Beirut.

It was a relief to leave Teheran, and the new city

seemed friendly. For my thirtieth birthday, which was not long after we arrived, I chartered a boat with the others in the office and we cruised up the coast towards Sidon. It was glorious. There was nothing festering here, I thought, as the waves sparkled around us.

The illusion lasted for two or three years and then things started to slide.

I was now alert to the signs. First, the rich started to leave, the rich always seeming to know the worst before the rest of us do. Second, the traders and merchants grew uninterested in paper currency and obsessed instead with gold. Third, guns began to appear, in the glove compartments of friends' cars and in the bureaus beside their telephones.

Prospero Import–Export moved out three months before the Israeli invasion. We went to Nicosia for a few months, full of smog and shops selling ancient Greek fertility figures with huge phalluses, before finally settling in Riyadh.

How would I describe it? It was hotter and more alien than the other places. I remember parties of hunters riding out of the city in big cars, the hawks and falcons perching on their arms; the outflow pipes from the oil wells burning orange in the night; and the desert like the sea, stretching in waves into the distance.

All this I liked. What I didn't like was what everyone complains about; that I had to have a male escort if I wanted to go shopping; that I couldn't drive; and that we weren't meant to drink.

Yet I could have been happy if I'd had my friends out there, for in their company the strangeness would have outweighed the restrictions. The trouble was, Zeeta hated Riyadh so much she left within a month; Sarah was moved back to Nicosia to run the new branch of Prospero Import–Export which we opened; and Pam met a Sri Lankan air steward and spent so much time with him she was as good as gone.

I lasted scarcely a year on my own. Then I packed it up and came back to England. It was 1983. Apart from when I'd been home on holidays, I'd been away for thirteen years. I was thirty-four years old.

4

The first thing I noticed when I came home were the politicians. They were on a crusade and we were all supposedly with them. Malingering and scrounging, cadging and shirking, were the evils they were intent on rooting out. Hard work and enterprise, efficiency and discipline, were the qualities they were going to put in their place.

Like the bearded ones, the Fundamentalists I had left behind, they were zealots. They had the truth, like the other lot had God, and they were as blind as each other.

I lived in the Kensington Gate Hotel, a boarding-house where you could rent a room by the week.

It was a large, rambling, somewhat decrepit building, with the stucco on the outside coming away in big pieces, like icing from a cake, a hallway table piled high with letters for tenants who had been gone for over twenty years, and dingy stair-wells which permanently smelt of cat.

I was on the fifth floor, with the communal bathroom on the other side of the landing. There was a crack in the lavatory seat and one had to be very careful sitting down that one didn't get pinched by it.

My room had been made by dividing up a much larger room, and through the partition walls I could hear my neighbours. One was a Lithuanian Baptist who prayed hoarsely for hours each night and whom I used to see in the street sometimes, hurrying along in a long black coat. The other was a Colombian, an illegal immigrant, who lived in dread of the police. He was an office-cleaner and he got up every morning at four o'clock. His wife was a diabetic and he was working to support her. We became friends and I used to help him with the international operator when he made his calls home. I gave him money once to send his wife some flowers on her birthday.

The room I had was small, with a narrow bed. The only other pieces of furniture were a wobbly bedside table and a wardrobe with 'Made in Taiwan' stamped on the back of it. The catch was broken and I had to wedge the door shut with a piece of cardboard.

There was a window which unfortunately only opened a few inches. Looking out from it what I saw was a small sheet of lead roofing where pigeons strutted about, the branch of a plane tree with its flat green leaves, and the Gloucester Road with traffic rumbling along it.

It was Zeeta who came to my rescue.

On returning a year before I did, she had started working for an accommodation agency, and by the time I was in the Kensington Gate Hotel she was running the office.

When she heard that a client, Mr Feldman, had an unfurnished flat to rent, she put us in touch.

29

*   *   *

I met him outside Westbourne Mansions and followed him into the courtyard.

'Isn't it continental,' I said, as I looked at the balconies rising around us, which was ridiculous because what it actually looked like was any old Peabody Trust building.

Mr Feldman said nothing, and the anxiety I felt about not getting the flat increased. As soon as I had seen over the place, I gave him two hundred pounds on the spot and I didn't ask for a receipt.

About a year after I moved in, Zeeta came to me with a proposal.

Rudi was a pole. She described him as good-looking and athletic. He was the friend of a friend of a friend, she said. Rudi wanted to stay in Britain. Would I consider marrying him for two thousand pounds.

It was winter, I had just finished with Claus, and I was not myself, I would say. I was in pain. So no sooner had Zeeta finished than I heard myself saying yes. Was it for the money? It would be a lie if I didn't admit I was being greedy at that moment, and I think like many people in the same situation, I fell for an offer which promised me money without having to do anything for it. But I think it was more the case that I wanted to do something – this is what I like to think anyway, although it is so difficult to disentangle it all – I think it is more the case that I wanted to do something, anything, absolutely anything at that moment, which would fill my time. I'd have taken any straw, and this was the one that just happened to be the first to come along.

Then I started to see the problems. Would I actually have to live with Rudi? No, Zeeta told me, I wouldn't. Would I have to sleep with him? Certainly not.

The only difficulty which Zeeta could foresee was the Home Office snoopers. For two years after the wedding – which would have to be a proper one to satisfy the authorities – we would have to be very careful to give the impression we were living together as man and wife. Mr Feldman would have to be told of my change of marital status and my surname would have to be changed on the lease. The entry in the telephone directory would need to be altered to read Mr and Mrs So-and-So. A little plate with the new name might even have to go up outside the front door. And so on.

Throughout this time we would live separately, of course. Then, after two years, we would divorce. It would be part of the contract that Rudi would see to that. I wouldn't even have to go to court. Then I'd be single again and I could marry whoever I wanted.

5

I met Rudi for the first time in a Chubbies sandwich bar near Waterloo, one Saturday morning.

I opened the door and he was sitting there, waiting. A woman with long earrings and a long face to match them was washing the floor with disinfectant.

We sat on high stools at the counter. I told him I didn't eat in the morning and he thought I was saying that I was hungry. He insisted on buying me a granary bap with egg mayonnaise in it. Rudi drank black coffee without sugar. As Zeeta had said, he was good-looking and athletic.

He told me his story. In Poland he had been a translator and he had had what he called 'a small career'. Because of the economic and political situation, he had always wanted to come west.

After much difficulty, he had finally managed to wangle it. Then, as soon as he had arrived in England, he had begun asking if he could live here permanently. The Home Office had umhed and ahed for several years, and although they hadn't said no categorically, the writing was on the wall.

However, if I married him, he said, they would have

to let him stay. And for helping him, he would give me two thousand pounds, half in advance and the rest after the ceremony. He was a good man, he promised me, and Zeeta would vouch for him.

I listened and stared into his eyes which were blue and faintly hypnotic. I've always thought blue eyes somehow meant people were honest, truthful and straightforward, although I've no reason to believe that's the case.

Then I heard myself saying that so long as he sorted out the divorce and the paperwork, I would marry him and I didn't want the money.

Why did I say this? Because I was desperate. Only I didn't know it and he certainly couldn't have guessed. He believed my offer was the action of a good Samaritan and his eyes filled with tears.

We said goodbye. He went back to the building site where he was working and I went to Waterloo. I was going home to Sussex for the weekend.

'You look cheerful,' said the clerk, as he whizzed me my ticket on the turntable.

'I've just got engaged,' I said, and then I added, remembering where I was going, 'I'm going home to tell my mother.'

'I'm happy for you,' the clerk called after me as I walked off, 'very, very happy.'

I was happy for myself, I have to say.

33

6

Of course at first, my mother did not approve of my getting married. My sister Vicki didn't approve either but at least she kept it to herself, while my mother, as usual, did not.

'I have no intention of coming – it's not for real,' were her words.

But then, with all the talk of what I would wear and the party afterwards and with going to buy the ring and all the rest of it, she began to think that the daughter she had long wished would settle down and start a family really was about to do this. It was not so much a change of heart she underwent, as that she started believing it was for real. I went through the same process, only I didn't realize it was happening.

There were two facts about the Registry Office which I immediately noticed when I went in: the walls were exactly the same colour as Heinz mushroom soup, and the traffic outside was making the windows rattle in their frames.

I was wearing a blue dress of crêpe-de-chine which I had bought in Beirut, and a hat with a short veil which I had borrowed from Zeeta. I had managed not to bite my nails for a fortnight and they were painted holly-red, same as my lipstick.

Rudi wore a navy blazer with a striped red-and-blue tie which he had bought in the King's Road. His only guest was an old uncle from Wembley, a man with huge grey eyebrows and brooding dark eyes. All his immediate family were dead and he wasn't close to his more distant relatives in Poland.

The guests who were standing behind us were therefore all my friends: there was Zeeta; there was Pam and her husband Peter, the air steward, and Jason, their three-year-old; there was Sarah and her young boyfriend, Malcolm, a scene-shifter in a theatre; there was Ron and his boyfriend, an accountant for Post Office Counters; there was Mr Anstruther with his wife Polly; there was my sister Vicki, Arthur her husband, and their twins, Cherry and Amanda; and there was my mother.

The Registrar started with a few words about the seriousness of marriage, after which Rudi had to repeat the words, and then it was my turn. As I said them, I noticed I was feeling odd.

Arthur, who was acting as best man, produced the ring from his waistcoat pocket and Rudi slipped it on to my finger. It was cold and again I felt odd.

Then the Registrar nodded, a sly grin on his face of the sort one has seen a hundred times in a hundred films. Rudi and I turned to each other. We'd only ever shaken hands before. I lifted my head. Our mouths touched and we kissed and I felt odd once more.

Then the Registrar pressed a button, a badly recorded cassette of the *Wedding March* started to play and the feeling vanished.

Rudi and I exited first. The corridor outside was lined with marble columns and smelt of linoleum polish. Half a dozen paces from the door there was a big woman with freckles and skin like raw sausage. She was surrounded by several young children and was talking to an official.

'This is not the Housing Department,' I heard him saying to her, 'This is Births, Marriages and Deaths.' He spoke slowly, as if he was talking to a foreigner.

'But I have nowhere to live,' replied the woman, sounding to my ears like an Irish gypsy.

'Hurry up,' I whispered to Rudi.

As we passed the gypsy's children, they stared at us with surprised and puzzled expressions, and then we passed through the next set of doors and we were gone.

Outside it was a raw, blustery spring day. As Ron arranged us for the wedding photographs on the steps, we had to hold on to our hats and our skirts as they fluttered. I noticed that all the bright yellow daffodils in all the window-boxes on the sills of the Registry Office had been flattened by the wind, and I knew then that this moment – the wind, the steps, these flowers – was going to be another in the series of memories which, run together, make up the story of my life.

After the photographs were finished, I threw my bouquet in the air. Ron caught it and everybody laughed. He divided the flowers between my nieces, telling them that because they were sharing, they would both be lucky.

There had been a lot of discussion about where to go

on to for the reception. My suggestion was a Polish restaurant next door to South Kensington underground station, which I had often passed by but never been into. Rudi loathed the idea. Cabbage and bad vodka was all we'd get, he'd said, and besides, he was trying to get away from Poland.

Zeeta suggested a Thai restaurant whose owner was a friend of hers. We plumped for it.

The King of Siam was in a house in Kilburn. Inside, we found a room with red wallpaper which smelt of rice and was cold despite the Calor gas heater blasting away in the corner. But then we all drank a few glasses of champagne, grew tipsy and forgot about where we were and the stains on the tablecloths.

Then a waitress in national costume ushered us down a rickety set of stairs. The basement was dark and lit with candles, and the walls were decorated with posters from Thai state airlines.

We ate sticks of satay and little sticky cubes of rice. There were speeches and toasts. Mother cried.

It was gone one o'clock when we rose. Upstairs was now filled with lunchtime customers who stared at us as we filed through in our best clothes.

We went back to Westbourne Mansions. Mother had made dishes of canapés; Ritz crackers with false caviar; cubes of cheese with chunks of pineapple; cold cocktail sausages which had been baked in honey.

As everyone started talking and drinking, I suddenly felt happy. I kicked off my shoes and carried the plates around in my stockinged feet. Ron saw that I have very large bunions and told me to rub lemon juice on them at night.

Rudi sat by the window, smoking a cigar and staring

at the Westway. You can see it curving in the distance from my flat, and day and night you can hear the cars as they speed along. The noise is a bit like the sea. I gave him a hug and he hugged me back.

This was the moment Zeeta presented her gift. It was a telephone answering machine and everyone gathered round to listen to Rudi and me as we recorded a message, speaking simultaneously: 'Hello, you've got through to Mr and Mrs Janowski. Our answering machine is always on, whether we are in or out. So if you'd like to leave your name and telephone number, we'll get back to you as soon as possible . . .'

The guests left in the evening, all of them light-headed from drinking all day. Mother helped me wash up the plates and the glasses and then went home with my sister. Rudi and I found ourselves alone.

Rudi was admiring the gold cross around my neck. I felt excited. He unzipped the back of my dress and took it off. He said something – he later told me it was the Polish for 'wife' – which I didn't take in. He took off my stockings and my underwear and I led him to the bedroom.

The sheets were cold when I got between them and that sobered me up. What are you doing, I asked myself. I wanted . . . I hardly dared admit it to myself.

Rudi was sitting on the edge of the bed taking off his shirt. His nipples were very small and the muscles of his chest very tight. He slid in beside me.

This is just fun, I remember thinking to myself, so don't take it seriously.

After we had made love, we were both wide awake. Rudi got up and found half a bottle of sweet white wine left over from the party. He mixed it with soda water and ice and we watched *From Here to Eternity* on the television.

A fortnight later Rudi came with his cardboard suitcase and a bunch of white roses, and we started living together. I was thirty-six years old and he was twenty-nine.

7

Rudi came from a village near the Russian border. It was a small place, surrounded by marshes, lagoons and groves of alder trees. In summer mosquitoes swarmed everywhere, while in wintertime the wind roared in from the east. His earliest memory, he told me, was finding a duck frozen in some pond ice; it was quite dead, yet because of its position it looked as if it were swimming along.

His mother died when he was an infant – tuberculosis, like my friend in Teheran, a tiny coincidence and one of many in my life. (It's a matter of knowing to look for them, isn't it? They're everywhere once you start.) His father remarried but then died of lung cancer when Rudi was a teenager.

This left Rudi with the stepmother. Her name was Sophia and she was a Protestant. Her cheeks were red and her nose was pointed, he used to say of her. Her own children were grown up and had left home. Relations between stepmother and stepson were cordial but not affectionate or loving.

Rudi studied hard, played basketball and nurtured hopes of being selected to play for the Polish national team. Unfortunately, he only grew to be six foot, so he had had to abandon that dream.

He left school at eighteen and went straight on to military service, which was compulsory. The training camp was in an old palace where the ceilings were painted white and gold, with cherubs and nymphs. The latrines were behind the stables, a long line of wooden O's over a ditch, where rats with bright eyes scurried amidst the filth.

When basic training was over, he wangled a job in transport – he had a talent for this kind of negotiation – and became a chauffeur. He drove a Zil, the Soviet answer to the Cadillac, a huge car which rode the roads like a ship cresting the waves.

The man he drove was a General who always carried a flask of ready-mixed martini, and liked to give lifts to attractive women. If the liquor took effect and the General got lucky, Rudi would park the Zil in some quiet spot and go for a long walk. The General tipped him handsomely for his discretion.

And when he wasn't driving or walking, Rudi and the other chauffeurs were stealing petrol from the army and selling it on the black market. It was the start of a lifelong habit.

When his tour of duty was up, Rudi went back to his studies. At the age of twenty-five, he graduated with a degree in linguistics. His special subject was English. He got a job as a translator in a state mineral company but was bored by the work, and besides, he was not paid enough. To make ends meet he 'liberated' geological samples and sold them illegally. His stepmother died. He thought Poland was a backward police state

41

run by incompetents.

One day, when he was in the office, he opened an old grey filing cabinet which had been badly loaded and it toppled over and fell on him. As he went backwards he hit the corner of a desk, chipping one of his vertebrae. An hour or two later, while he was in hospital waiting to go into the X-ray room, he made his decision. He was leaving Poland. For ever.

He came to Britain, rather than any other country, because he had a relative here – his bachelor uncle in Wembley. This was his real mother's much older brother, who had been a member of the Free Polish Air Force and stayed behind after the war.

For his first four years in London, Rudi worked in restaurants and on building sites where he was paid cash in hand, no questions asked. Then we met and married, and after that Rudi was able to take his first proper job. It was with a security firm based at Heathrow. Half the time he checked warehouses where goods were stored around the airport, and the other half he worked in the terminals, checking hand-luggage and passengers.

One evening I came home and found he was back from work before me. He had a box of electric clocks and he was filing the numbers off the backs of them. He explained to me that he had found them in a bin at work.

An hour later the front door bell rang and Rudi went out to answer it. After a whispered conversation in the hall he returned with a man he introduced to me as Mr Hodges. He was a man in his fifties who wore Brylcreem in his hair, was troubled by an ulcer, and kept one hand permanently under his jacket on his stomach, for comfort.

Mr Hodges gave Rudi a large wad of cash and carried the clocks away, and from then on there was no end to the cigarettes, clothes, stereos and so on that Rudi brought home from work, goods apparently unwanted, damaged, or surplus to requirements. He kept them in my wardrobe or in a space under the floorboards he'd worked loose in the living-room.

At first I didn't like it and when I told him, he told me to mind my own business. I went on complaining, although with little effect, and there wasn't anything else that I could do. I was hardly going to report him. Then I grew used to it. He only takes a little, he's careful and he's not greedy, I thought. Finally, I grew blasée, and Mr Hodges counting notes into Rudi's hand became a fixture, like the trip to the supermarket for the weekly shop on Saturday mornings. You can grow accustomed to anything if it happens to you often enough.

Once I'd accepted Rudi's sideline, I let him take charge of our finances completely. He had a good attitude to money. He put aside what was needed for rent or bills, and the rest he spent and he spent freely.

He always took us out to dinner when we could afford it and there was always wine. He bought me a Liberty scarf and a mauve cashmere sweater. He bought me a hair-dryer. He bought me a lovely manicure set in a real kid case.

It sounds as if I'm saying I loved him because he bought me things, but it would have been just the same between us if we'd had no money. The reason I bring these things up is because they connect us. They are, in fact, apart from a few notes he wrote and the photographs I have, the only things I have that connect us, and when I want to feel him, it is to them I have turned. Holding the scarf, touching the manicure set, I am able to conjure up the feeling of him in a way that is impossible otherwise, and to such an extent it is almost as if he were with me. His presents are my link back. It's easier talking about them than describing what we had. How does one put that into words? I will try.

After we had been married about a year and a half, I remember Zeeta called round one evening.

'How would you describe him?' she asked.

'Dependable,' I said, and went on to explain how Rudi was a man of regular habits, who came home when he said, took me out when he said and always did what he said he would do.

As we talked, another word floated into my head. It was 'bonus'. That's what it was, I continued, a bloody bonus.

Somewhere along the line I'd done a good deed, and now I was being rewarded. I had been given a companion who wasn't going to stray from my side, and with whom I was going to grow old. He also wanted to have a child, like I did. All this I told Zeeta.

Next thing Rudi came back from work. He was wearing his blue serge uniform and the hat with 'Vanguard Security' above the peak. I kissed him and went to find my lipstick.

'We've been talking about you,' I heard Zeeta saying as I came back into the room. 'We think you're a pretty special guy.' She said it in a fake American accent, as

44

Zeeta often does when she wants to say something important.

Rudi shrugged and returned the compliment. 'I love her,' he said.

While I heard these words I felt a funny feeling inside. It was desire. It was happiness. It was also like the sensation you get on the Big Wheel when it starts to drop.

I loved someone, who in turn loved me, and we were going to have a child. Or at least we were going to try.

'Fancy a bottle of something?' said Zeeta. 'I thought I'd nip over to the off-licence.'

After she slipped out I said, 'I wish we could go to bed.'

'And we will,' said Rudi, 'later. We will anticipate what is coming as we drink and that will make the end of the evening all the more exciting.'

I was happy. I spoke the words 'I love you too' into his crinkly ear.

Two

8

The suit which I bought for Brighton was a brown tweed with white flecks and lined with silk. It came from Frock Swop, and when I spotted it hanging in the window, it looked brand-new.

'She only wore it once,' said the proprietress, referring to the previous owner, 'then decided she didn't like the buttons.'

These were bone, white with black marbling and with beautiful smooth rims.

'But then, if you've got the money, you can do what you like, can't you? And she's got health and good looks as well, but then, don't they always go with money?'

We laughed together as I fished out my purse. She was a long-faced woman with two small eyes which gave her the look of a currant bun. She folded the jacket inside out and said, slipping it into a Frock Swop bag, 'My husband always says there's a difference in this world between cash and money, you know. Now you and me – that'll be ninety, dear – all we ever have is cash.'

I handed her two fifties.

'Here one week, gone the next. See, you've just said goodbye to a hundred. Now, money is different. Those who have it always seem to end up with more and more of it because somehow, in their hands, it grows. Haven't you noticed?'

She handed me back my change.

'There's your ten but it won't last, will it? It'll be gone by the time you're home. You think about what I've said.'

We laughed again . . .

Looking at the suit as it hung in my wardrobe I remembered the conversation, and coming home that day and trying on the suit and noticing the strong smell of perfume that clung to the collar, and deciding to have it cleaned.

I lifted the hanger down from the rail, pulled off the polythene and the room was suddenly filled with that spirit smell of something dry-cleaned.

A distant sound of clattering made me look up, and I wondered if it was a pot lid. When we first lived together Rudi used to amaze me with his ability to recognize sounds from other flats, and I've caught the habit from him. He had acquired the skill in Poland where, with all the walls being made of paper, as he puts it, everything was audible.

One would have assumed that on coming west, he would have wanted to escape from the noises of others, but he loved them. A neighbour's noises said to him, 'Life's going on', and he always hoped that his, in their turn, were being heard by others. For that way, he said, others would know he was living as well, and I know now exactly what he meant, better than I understood then.

*　　*　　*

I took off my skirt and jacket and stood in front of the mirror. Then I took off the rest of my clothes.

My legs are short and a bit bandy and on one knee, which I could clearly see, there is a big white scar which wiggles like a snake. The cause of it was Vicki pushing me off a garden chair. This happened when I was four.

I can still remember the moment as I flew through the air and saw the rake lying on the lawn, its spikes pointing upwards. There were a few white daisy heads in the grass, and birdsong, and I knew that an accident was inevitable.

I've never been able to recall the next part, when the spikes went into my leg. I remember nothing until I'm on my father's knee. The cut is deep and there's a great flap of skin hanging down over it. There is blood streaming out which he is mopping up with cotton-wool balls. When they're soaked and useless, he throws them into an enamel bowl on the grass.

I watch the pile growing higher and higher. The fresh blood is vividly red, almost the colour of a pillar-box, but when it has dried it goes brown, the same as our water I think, after it has lain in our pipes for a while.

Eventually my dad says we must go to the hospital. He drives me there in his black car. Inside the red-brick building I'm put on a hard bed with a green curtain drawn around it. A coloured doctor appears gives me a boiled sweet and says, 'Oh dear, oh dear, oh dear,' reminding me of the White Rabbit in *Alice in Wonderland*. I need four stitches. I have no recollection of any pain . . .

I pulled on the skirt and then the jacket and looked

into the mirror. It hung well. Then I looked at my face. I have a wide forehead and as I wear my hair without a fringe, it shows. I have a largish mouth but my lips are a little too thin for my liking. I have a strong nose and a rounded chin. My eyes are almond-shaped and brown. My auburn hair is wispy and thin and I wear it long, often tying it at the back with a big crêpe bow.

When I don't like myself I think my face looks the way a child draws but I was feeling cheerful then and saw that I was looking good. Rudi said of my face that it was permanently changing and that he could always tell my mood from my expression.

I turned round and had a backwards look over my shoulder. The jacket hung nicely and the hem of the skirt was straight, just over the back of my knees. I had been wondering about shoes and at that moment I remembered I had some flat velvet pumps with small bows. I opened the drawer at the bottom of the wardrobe and, as I dug them out, the doorbell rang. It was not a cheerful little ring which a friend would give, nor was it the familiar kind which Rudi sometimes gave, in order not to give me a fright coming in. It was a long ring, determined, and it said, 'This is official.'

I padded across the bedroom in my bare feet and out to the hall. Behind the glass in the front door I saw two dark shapes. They said it again: 'This is official. Open the door.'

I undid the latch cautiously. On the doorstep outside stood a police constable and a policewoman.

Rudi's been caught, I thought, and in my mind's eye the very next instant I saw my future as a prisoner's wife, told in pictures taken from television and newspapers. I saw a prison gate with a little door set in it, exactly the same as the way into Westbourne Mansions, and I was stepping through it. I saw prisoners' wives queueing before warders. They were dressed in their best clothes and holding bawling children. I was there in my tweed suit, of course. I saw a crowded room with wire mesh running down the middle, and Rudi was on one side with the prisoners, while I was on the other with the dolled-up wives.

Mixed up with all this was a photograph in a newspaper I had seen at some point as a child, and which had made a tremendous impression on me. It was of the crowd outside Wandsworth prison, waiting for news of Bentley's hanging.

'Is this the residence of Mrs Jan-o-ska?' the policewoman asked.

'Janowski, yes.'

'Are *you* Mrs Janowski?'

'I am.'

'May we come in?'

I stared at the policewoman's face.

Don't keep me in agony, tell me now, I thought, but what I heard myself saying was, 'Of course, of course, come in.'

I led the way down the hall to the living-room at the back of the flat. The fireplace lies behind the door as you come in, and the two windows are opposite. The foreground view is mainly of grey slate roofs; then in the middle distance are the railway tracks which run into Paddington station; and then finally, in the far distance, stretches the Westway.

My heart was pounding and panic was racing through me. It was filling my middle, the pressure outwards was getting stronger and stronger, and I was going to burst with it.

What in God's name is it, I wanted to shout, except I couldn't possibly have done that, my throat being jammed.

The policewoman held her little fist in front of her little mouth and coughed. Her cap was tucked under the other arm. The policeman was watching her.

'Look,' he said, and then I knew. It was one tiny little word occupying one tiny little bit of time, but I could tell from the way he said it, the way he was standing, the shifty look in his eyes, he had come to tell me something far more awful than what I imagined that first moment when I'd opened the door to them.

'I'm afraid, Mrs Janowski, something has happened and your husband . . . has died.'

I heard those curious words 'has died' and for a very short moment I wondered, What does that mean? it didn't last long, I can assure you.

At once I thought, It isn't true. It can't be. There's been some mistake.

'You should sit down,' said the policeman.

Would I like to sit down, I wondered. This must be the only situation in the world where a complete stranger can come into your house and suggest you sit down in your own living-room.

'Yes,' I said, and we all sat. The policeman took the hard chair by the sideboard, the policewoman took the armchair near the fireplace, and I perched on the arm of the other armchair.

'There must be some mistake,' I repeated and I shook my head.

'Mrs Janowski,' the policewoman began. There was a small spot under her mouth which she was nervously rubbing with her thumb.

'It is always very difficult to accept and understand, I do know, news which has come so suddenly like this.'

The policeman was watching her like a hawk, and his two enormous nostrils were dark circles in the middle of his face.

'But what happened?'

'We don't know exactly. Your husband was in a car and he had some sort of fatal attack. Heart or something.'

My stomach seemed to split open and fall away. I shook my head emphatically. 'I'm afraid that's not possible. That's absolutely not possible.'

It couldn't be. I had bought my suit. We were going to Brighton. We were going to visit the Royal Pavilion. We were going to have lunch with my mother on Sunday. We had even arranged for the taxi to her house.

'There's been a mistake,' I said. 'You've mixed him up with someone else. He's at Heathrow now.'

'There isn't any doubt about it,' said the policeman. 'It is Mr Janowski, your husband, that we're talking about.'

'We could telephone and get confirmation,' said the policewoman very quietly. She lifted her straw-coloured hair out of her eyes and I saw they were wet.

'Do you mind if we use your telephone, Mrs Janowski?' asked the policeman coldly, staring at his colleague.

'Please ring,' I said, and in my mind's eye I saw again the crowd waiting outside Wandsworth for news of Bentley's hanging.

It was as the policeman turned towards the telephone that I remembered the bloody thing was stolen.

Oh my God! What else is there, I thought, and I started racing round the room in my imagination. Oh dear – self-assembly rocking-chair, Swedish glass candlesticks, cork table mats, the two bottles of Jim Beam in the sideboard, the Moulinex in the kitchen. . . . The list went on and on but at that point I gave up.

'I'm with Mrs Janowski now,' I heard the policeman saying. 'I'm in her flat.'

This was followed by several 'umhs' and 'ahs' until finally, the policeman said, 'I wonder, Mrs Janowski if you wouldn't mind speaking?'

I put the receiver to my hot ear. The voice at the other end floated into me.

'Would the hair be a light brown, almost fair, would you say?'

'Yes,' I heard myself agreeing, but surely, I thought, there must be some mistake . . .

'Would there be a mole on the left hand, on the last knuckle of the little finger?'

'Yes,' I heard myself agreeing, but surely I thought, there must be some . . .

'There's an English-Polish dictionary with Rudi Janowski, Warsaw, 1981, written in the flyleaf. Would that have been your husband's?'

'Yes,' I heard myself agreeing, but surely I thought, there must be . . .

No, there was no mistake, I put down the telephone and felt the pain. It was as if my chest had been torn open, something boiling hot poured in, and then sewn up again. It was like a raging heartburn but I knew then it was a heartburn for which there was neither cure nor relief. It was in me and I would never get it out. Even then I realized the best I could hope for was that something hard would form around it like the hard skin on the heels of the feet, which might deaden the feeling.

'Would you like a cup of tea?' asked the police-woman.

I suddenly felt a great surge of anger towards them. For those few moments before I'd taken the phone, I had actually believed there had been a mistake. Or I'd half-believed it anyway and hope had briefly flourished. Then the worst had been confirmed and now I was left feeling worse than I would have been had I not hoped. So why the hell hadn't the police been more convincing to begin with, I wondered. None of this would have happened otherwise. And all this in less time than it takes to blink.

'Just point me towards the milk, Mrs Janowski, and I'll be able to manage,' the policewoman continued.

'No,' I cried, 'I'll make the tea,' and walked quickly out.

In the kitchen I took the lid off the kettle and carried it over to the sink. As the water splashed from the tap the descaler inside tossed about like something in the sea. I carried the kettle back to the socket and turned it on. Then I used the tea-towel to dry the tears off my face. It smelt faintly of milk and tea and sugar, and I remembered Rudi took sugar with his tea but not with his coffee.

I lifted the tray from the top of the unit where it lives, took a small white cloth out of the drawer where I kept my good things and spread it out. Then I put out my best cups, a jug of milk, and a little bowl of sugar and some spoons. Finally, I poured some digestive biscuits from the biscuit barrel on to the plate with parrots painted around the edge, and that went on to the tray as well.

I cupped my hands around the kettle. It was luke-warm, not yet hot.

My kitchen lies along the side of the flat. The cupboards are white and there is a grey enamelled gas stove on black legs. The floor is uneven and Rudi levelled the stove with pieces of matchbox.

In front of the window there is a Belfast sink, white

58

and deep, and there are patches of green on the old taps. A big rounded fridge stands in the other corner. It always smells faintly of gas when you open the door and it hums loudly in the night. The rubber sealant is old and worn and every morning there is water in a little puddle on the floor in front.

A Sheila-maid hangs from the ceiling, below which stands the table, a dark heavy piece with folding leaves. Rudi bought it one Sunday morning in Brick Lane. It cost twenty pounds. It was so heavy, we had to bring it home in a taxi, which was another twenty, and so what was to have been a cheap table turned out not to be. Then we discovered it wasn't even comfortable to sit at; its legs are always in the way. I pulled out a chair and sat down.

Through the window I looked out at another kitchen in the next block. A nice-looking woman was sitting at her table. She was reading and a cigarette burned in her hand.

I had a strangely calm thought about all the lives that go on around each other all the time, unnoticed. She may have wept in her kitchen for all I knew, I thought, and yet I'd never seen.

As the kettle started to boil, the lid lifted and dropped. I got up and poured the hot water into the teapot. With the steam which drifted up there came the smell of freshly made tea, and I put my head into the cloud and drank it in, and the next moment I had this uncanny sense of seeing myself as I was doing it.

I gripped the tray and carefully walked out. Something terrible had happened but, if I could just go on, I might be all right. If I could just go on.

I was gripping the tray so hard, my knuckles were

white by the time I had set it down on the table next door, by the windows.

'I must ring my sister, Vicki,' I announced to the police.

When I told her the news, my sister screamed and yet her shout sounded as if it came from the far end of a tunnel.

Arthur, Vicki's husband, came to the telephone then and said, 'We'll put the kids next door and be over as soon as we can.'

I remembered one of Rudi's stories. The icicles at the end of the Polish winter, hanging from the eaves of houses, and children snapping them off to make swords. Sometimes the icicles fell from tall buildings and speared people through the tops of their heads. One of them had fallen and it had caught me and I was speared on to the snow . . .

I put down the telephone and said, 'Would you mind waiting until my sister arrives?'

'Not at all,' said the policeman.

He had stood up from his chair, put his helmet down and was advancing towards me.

'Shall I be Mother?' he asked, picking up the teapot.

10

The tea was poured. We sat down. I said I wanted to go to the hospital. I wanted to see Rudi straight away. They advised me against it. They asked if I would wait and I found myself agreeing.

Then we sat together without speaking. The only sounds were of cups scraping on saucers, and sips of tea going down our throats.

That was when a syrupy, tranced feeling crept over me and I began to daydream . . .

I was in a strange, empty space that was filled by a thick, dense mist. Yet I moved confidently, without fear of falling or tripping, for I could feel the surface underfoot was as smooth as stainless steel and I knew it stretched away for ever.

As I padded forward I passed dark shapes which I recognized as trees and carts. Then I heard voices. They were soft and muffled and I couldn't tell how far away they were, nor could I make any sense of what they were saying.

I pointed myself in their direction but then the voices seemed to be coming from yet a third direction.

I gave up searching – I would inevitably bump into

the source of the voices, I reasoned – and walked on. And that was when I grew certain Rudi was going to appear, and I started wondering when this was going to be. I began to look around for him. I started listening for the sound of his voice and I was filled with a sense of anticipation and certain that at any moment he would be there. Then into my mind there suddenly came a desperate longing for a cigarette . . .

The world of mist and whispers vanished and I was back in my living-room, in the world of cups scraping on saucers.

'Do you by any chance have a cigarette?' I asked.

'Sorry, no,' said the policeman.

The policewoman shook her head and said, 'I haven't had one for six months, I'm sorry.'

I tried my neighbour Wendy next door, but she was out. But I had to have one, so I would have to go to the shops. I went back into my flat and took my coat from its hook in the hall. As I pulled it on I could hear the police talking animatedly in the living-room. When I had been with them they had not been able to talk, but now I was gone there was no stopping them.

'I'm going to take the plaster down from around my fireplace,' I heard the policeman saying, 'and leave the brickwork exposed.'

'That'll look nice,' said the policewoman.

I found my purse. It is black, with my initials on the front, C.J. Rudi had given it to me for my thirty-ninth birthday.

'I'd like to paint the lounge walls magnolia, but the wife wanted something with a bit more cream in it.'

I put my head around the door and said, 'I'm just going out to buy some cigarettes.'

62

'Shall I walk down with you?' offered the police-woman, standing up and smoothing the front of her skirt.

'No, thank you.' That was the last thing I wanted, to be seen in the street with her.

'I'll only be a minute,' I said.

'Have you thought about acacia?' I heard the police-woman saying as I went down the hall.

I went out and shut the door and her voice was gone.

11

I walked up Queensway as far as the Wineways off-licence, opened the door and went in. The Sikh owner was asleep behind the counter. His long-haired Alsatian was dozing beside him. As the door shut behind me the dog woke up and came out.

'Excuse me,' I said loudly as I felt the dog's cold snout against my knee. Alsatians are not my strong point. Thank God, the next moment somebody came in, the bell rang, and the proprietor woke up and struggled to his feet.

'Come here, Susie,' he called to the dog and the cold nose came away from my leg.

As the dog trotted behind the counter, the Sikh yawned, stretched himself, then put on a sheepish look of apology.

'Yes,' he said, addressing a tall heavy man, forty-five to fiftyish and wearing a tweed coat, who was looking past me towards the shelves. The man wore spectacles and he had two widely spaced front teeth.

'Can I help you?'

'The lady's first,' said the man to the proprietor, and he beamed at me.

I bought twenty Marlboro and a box of matches. As I left I heard the man asking for a bottle of Irish whiskey.

I started walking back down Queensway. A few doors further on was the Blue Sky café. Through the glass, slightly misted with condensation, I could see its blue formica tables, figures bent over them eating their evening meals, and the huge neon lights that hang from the ceiling. At the back was the serving counter, the steaming Gaggia machine, and George the waiter reading his newspaper.

The police wouldn't miss me for a few more minutes, would they, I thought. I pushed open the door and went in. It was all familiar; the hum of the neon, the smell of cabbage and coffee, the clatter of knives and forks on plates, and someone singing in the kitchen.

I bought a cappuccino and went and sat at the only free table, which was in the corner. I opened my packet of Marlboro. After the first puff of my first cigarette in twelve months, my head started to spin. I balanced the cigarette on the edge of the old Senior Service ashtray and watched the smoke curling up from the end. It was grey, and the way it rumpled and dimpled reminded me of waves at sea.

'Excuse me, is anyone sitting here?'

It was an English voice, quite posh and pushy. I looked up. It was the customer from Wineways.

I thought, George is here, I'll be all right, and so I shrugged.

'Yes. Sit,' I said.

The man carefully placed the bottle he was carrying on the table and cautiously sat down.

'I've got two police in my flat down there,' I said, pointing outside.

'Oh yes, why's that?'

'They're waiting for me while I popped out.'

There was leather edging on his cuffs, the colour of chestnut. He undid the top button of his coat. His face was square and behind his glasses his eyes bulged slightly. They were green. He was unshaven and there was stubble on his face.

'You were in the off-licence, weren't you?'

'Yes.'

'I thought so.'

He pulled his coat open. Underneath he wore a jacket and a blue-and-white striped shirt with a green tie. He put his hands around his cup. He was drinking tea. His fingers were heavy and strong.

'Have you noticed that the evenings are getting longer?'

I looked up from his hands to his face.

'Yet it's still quite cold, isn't it? There's still a wintry feel around. And that's a funny thing about the weather,' he continued. 'It should be warm and summery now. It should be – to go with the fact that the evenings are quite long. But it isn't. And then, come August, we get the same thing only the other way round. The days are hot yet it gets dark early, for the evenings are already shortening for the winter . . .

'Isn't this British? Strangers meet in a café for the first time, and automatically they talk about the weather – that great conversational failsafe.'

I nodded and he said, 'Do you mind my being here?' and stared at me with his big green eyes.

Why should I, I thought. I didn't mind. I communicated this to him with a shrug.

We sat and we sipped. I noticed his body under his coat was square like his head and he looked strong.

'Have you ever been in Donegal in the summer?' he asked.

I shook my head.

'The evenings there are quite extraordinary. It hardly gets dark at all it's so far north and west . . .'

'My husband has just died,' I interrupted him. 'I came home from work tonight and they came to my flat and they told me. Just a little while ago.'

He stared, a little incredulous and suddenly a little nervous.

'We were going away on holiday, my husband and I, tomorrow, to Brighton. His name is Rudi. I came home and the police came to my flat. They said to me, "Your husband has died." He was at work this afternoon and something happened. His heart or something. And he died, just like that.

'I didn't believe it at first. So we rang the hospital. They had his Polish-English dictionary with his name in it. I identified it over the phone. There's no mistake. It was his all right. Can you believe that?

'I'm a widow; that's a funny word. It sounds like window but it isn't. You have to be old to be a widow, I've always thought. You have to be old, don't you? Am I old?'

He shook his head

'Yet I am a widow,' I said. 'Do I look like one?'

He shook his head again.

'I don't know if I feel like one yet. I don't know what I feel. This has only happened such a short while ago, I don't yet know what I feel.'

'I'm very sorry to hear about your trouble,' he said nicely.

There was a different look now. You see it whenever there's an accident or tragedy in the street. It's that set look of sympathy.

'You believe me?'

'Yes.'

'You didn't at first?'

He shrugged.

'You thought there was something funny about me.'

'No,' he said, not very convincingly.

'You came over to chat me up.'

He started to laugh and I started to laugh with him. We laughed together.

'Are you Italian?' I asked abruptly.

'Why do you ask? You're the first person who's ever asked me that question, ever. And actually, I am. My mother's mother was from Pisa. That makes me a quarter Italian.'

I could feel myself, as I looked at him, growing faintly hypnotized, and I felt certain it was the same for him. We were mesmerizing one another.

'You know,' he said, 'this is the first time I've ever done this – gone up to a table, complete stranger, introduced myself and sat down.'

I laughed.

'Before I came in here, when I stood on the pavement, I tried to think up something clever to say. But as always, when you're in this sort of situation, nothing came to me. So I decided on the straightforward approach. I would just come in and start speaking to you.

'But now I feel as if I've intruded on you. And if I had known what's just happened to you, I wouldn't have forced myself on you like I did.'

'But you didn't. I said you could sit down.'

'Has this ever happened to you before? Someone just coming up out of the blue and starting to talk to you? I'm certain strangers ask to sit at your table all the time.'

I tilted my head back and drank the milky top of the cappuccino out of the bottom of the cup.

'I have to go.'

'Oh yes. The police are waiting in your flat.'

'One's a policewoman.'

I felt this wave going through me. My eyes filled with tears and he stared at me.

'Are you all right?'

'Am I? Yes, I'm all right.'

Suddenly, it was as if he was someone I had known a long time.

'Are you sure?'

I thought, How soothing you sound.

'I'm terrified,' I said. 'This is only the start and I know it's going to be worse.'

'Like the sun, is it? You're terrified it'll scorch you.'

I thought, He understands me.

'I felt drawn to you in the off-licence,' he began.

He'd been going so well up to this point but now my heart sank.

'I must have sensed something about you . . .'

I wondered if he wanted to put his hand on my hand. It was lying on the blue formica surface of the table but he didn't try.

'I must have sensed something . . .'

'I have to go,' I said.

I expected him to get up when I stood but he didn't. Instead he quickly took something out of his pocket and pressed it into my hand.

'If you want to see me again,' he said, 'that would make me happy.'

I looked down and saw it was a card, a long, white oblong shape lying across the middle of my palm with black print in the middle.

I turned towards the door, wondering if he was going to try to say anything more, or if he was going to get up and try to open it for me, but he did neither.

Out on the pavement I glanced back. Through the glass I saw him sitting at the table, slightly blurred on account of the condensation. He raised his hand and gave me a brief wave and I raised my hand and waved back. Then I hurried on.

When I got to the corner the pedestrian light was red and I had to stop. I looked at the card which I was still holding:

John Pashley
Bookseller
35 Marlbank
PRIMROSE HILL
London NW3 5QT
01–586 4970

The pain was pressing in me and I sensed it had spread further since the last assessment. I think this was the worst part about that early evening, living with the knowledge that what was coming was going to get worse.

It was like, having seen your house burn to the ground, sitting down to wait for dark. You knew you were going to have to sleep all night in the open and yet you didn't have the slightest clue what that meant. The man in the café understood that.

The green signal man started flashing. I crossed the road and put the card into my purse, behind the picture of Rudi in the little plastic window. Then I put my purse into my pocket and hurried towards home, where the police were waiting, and where my sister and her husband would soon arrive.

12

The bell rang and the policewoman went to answer it. A moment later Vicki was in my living-room. I stood up and her arms wrapped around me. She wore a half-length jacket of fake fur. It had begun to spot with rain outside and where the collar touched my neck I felt it was sprinkled with drops of wet.

Arthur slipped into the room behind his wife, while simultaneously the policeman and policewoman picked up their helmets and started towards the door nodding goodbye, expressions on their faces for Arthur's benefit which said, 'Treat her carefully, she's about to break,' to which he did not respond.

I heard the front door banging shut as the police left, and separated myself from Vicki. Arthur was smiling and lifting something on to the table which I hadn't noticed him coming in with and which I now saw was the cat basket.

'We brought Tiff along,' he said. 'We thought perhaps she might cheer you up.'

I took a cigarette from the packet and lit it.

'You've started smoking again,' said Vicki quietly, hanging her coat over the door.

She stood in the middle of the floor looking down at her feet, just as she always has when she's thinking, even when she was a child, and I could see she was wondering whether to say something like, 'It was such a struggle giving up, Cath, don't start again,' and then Tiffany went, 'Miaow' inside her basket and she turned to the table.

'Poor little Tiffs,' she said, 'Mummy hasn't forgotton you.'

She undid the straps, pulled open the door and Tiffany slunk out. She is a grey-coloured, short-haired Burmese with yellow eyes and a bony body. She padded up to the window and stared out, her tail whisking to and fro, while cars with their headlamps burrowing through the darkness swept along the Westway in the distance.

There was rum in the fridge and we mixed it with Coca Cola. After two glasses I began to feel very much better. I held my glass out for Arthur to make a third. He took it to the kitchen. Tiffany was on my sister's lap. She dipped a finger into her glass of rum-and-coke and held it out. As the cat licked, I could hear her pink tongue scraping on Vicki's skin.

'Trying to get Tiffers drunk,' Arthur joked as he returned to the room, and Vicki laughed.

'Is Tiffers going to go and give Cath a cuddle?' my sister asked her cat, stroking her under the chin.

'I don't think I want Tiffany,' I said, rather more boldly than I meant to. I didn't like her crawling on my lap and digging her claws into my skin.

'What! But she's desperate to give you a kiss.'

'Didn't you hear?' said Arthur. 'She doesn't want her.'

73

Arthur comes from Bradford and he has never quite lost his accent. He works for Haringey Council. His hair was once blond but now is white, and though he is fifty-two it still grows thickly. After they married Vicki insisted he had the tattoos on his arms taken off. The operation left huge shiny scars which are far worse than the mermaid and the anchor which had been there before. Now he never bares his arms in public.

I was trying to find the words to explain I didn't want the cat when Vicki interrupted in her baby voice and said, 'Don't say anything nasty about Tiffers. She's very sensitive and she understands everything.'

'She is that,' agreed Arthur, turning to his wife. 'Do you remember that time we were burgled?'

He turned back to me.

'The buggers had made a terrible mess. Pulled everything off the shelves, crapped in the kitchen, you name it. Vicki and the twins were away at the time and the business completely knocked me for six. Didn't know where to begin cleaning up or what to do.

'That's when I hear the cat flap going "boing-boing", and into the living-room comes Tiffers. She looks around like she's saying, "Whey! What's this?" and then gets on to my lap, paws up on either shoulder, head against the cheek, and she gives me a cuddle. She's that understanding, she's like a real person.'

I began to laugh and went on laughing until little tears started to roll down my cheeks and I felt my muscles stretching down my sides.

Through the wet in my eyes I could see Arthur and Vicki looking across at me, and I could see they were thinking, Is she laughing at our story or is she drunk?

All the way from Epping they must have had a feeling of dread as well as shock, and now here we were, all happy together. Suddenly, they looked pleased with themselves and began to laugh with me and we didn't stop for what seemed like minutes.

Three

13

It was the next morning and in my mind the words formed as we drove along:

– Outside the window London glid past –

That's wrong, I thought – glides past – that was better – London glides past –

From the moment I'd woken up, from a deep and seemingly dreamless sleep, I hadn't been able to stop them. The words had just kept coming, like air bubbles in a fish-tank rushing to the surface, and inside my head they wrote themselves into a diary which described events within a moment of their happening.

'All right, Cathy?'

Vicki addressed the question to me. Vicki was in the front of the car, Tiffany's basket balanced on her lap. Arthur was driving.

The diary continued:

– Arthur drives carefully. He wears shades which clip on to his glasses. They make him look like an insect –

'Yes, I feel fine,' I said.

– 'I feel fine,' I say. In fact I feel crushed and trapped and I find it hard to breathe   I am in a panic about what is getting closer and closer –

'I think you're being very brave,' said Arthur.

– 'I think you're being very brave,' says Arthur   I've lost count how many times he has said this   From the basket comes the sound of Tiffany going 'Miaow'   I turn and look out of the car window   I hope we will all be quiet for the next few minutes –

We drove along the M4 towards the airport. From the flyover which runs like a rollercoaster along the level of the rooftops, I saw the old Lucozade clock tower. In the days when I travelled, the neon sign on the side used to read, 'Lucozade Aids Recovery'. Now those days are long gone.

A little further on stood the old Beecham's building. For me it was another landmark. The letters of the name gleamed like moonlight. Next door stood the new Wang building, glazed with chocolate-coloured glass and impossible to see into.

– Outside the car window, West London glides past   We pass a building which can't be seen into   People in business want to stare out at us in secret but never want to be seen themselves –

Arthur manoeuvred the car into a parking space. I opened my handbag and looked in the mirror. I saw I'd chewed off my lipstick during the drive.

I put my hand inside the bag. In the crinkly leather folds at the bottom I found a lipstick and ran it round my mouth. Then I looked back into the mirror and I asked myself the question, Why did you say 'Yes' to this?

Arthur had made the arrangements on the telephone the night before. In a short while, which is what I had

80

agreed to, I was going to identify Rudi's body. It was to be my last chance to see him. It was most likely going to be the worst of my ordeals, and once it was over the rest would be easier, I thought.

– Arthur turns off the ignition I wind up the window, open the door and get out Tiffany in her basket is put where I was sitting We can't bring her into the hospital I feel tired and frightened –

The moment when I was going to have to look at Rudi was getting closer and closer, I thought.

– My thighs tremble under my skirt They feel like water I can see daffodils in a window-box They are waving in the wind I remember the Registry Office and the day of my marriage –

I felt a great stab inside. There were objects waiting to trigger memories lurking round every corner, I realized.

– We start to walk in silence along the pavement Outside a newsagent's the previous days *London Standard* headline says something about rising interest rates Arthur sighs –

I thought of Rudi. I imagined he was waiting for me in a room, sitting on a chair and holding a glass. There was a cigarette between his fingers although he didn't smoke. His eyes were open. I stopped.

'Are you all right?' asked Arthur.

– 'Are you all right?' asks Arthur, and he looks as if there is something the matter with me –

– 'You've gone as white as a sheet,' says Vicki –

'You don't have to through with it, you know, if you don't want to,' said Arthur gently. 'I can do it, or Vicki can do it.'

But I want to, I thought, I have to, I ought to.

'I can identify him,' Arthur repeated, 'I'll do that.'

– He stares at me with his mild brown eyes   Why have I never noticed they are so mild before? –

I said, 'Where will Rudi be?'

'I don't exactly know,' he said cautiously. 'In some sort of a morgue, I should think.'

– I am terrified   I am excited   I won't admit it but I cling to a secret hope   It will not be Rudi when I get inside the hospital   It will be someone else and Rudi will be alive –

'I tell you what,' I heard Arthur saying, 'we'll see how you feel closer to the time.'

I nodded and we started walking on again.

14

The hospital corridors were shiny and smelt of wax, and there were signs everywhere hanging down from the ceiling, like in an international airport.

'Are you sure you can go through with this?'

Oh yes, I was sure I was sure. It'll be good for you, I told myself. You just have to keep thinking that. And I'd kept thinking it all the time we had been walking along the shiny hospital corridors.

Finally, we stopped in front of a big pair of doors set in an archway. It's going to be good for you, I told myself. You are going to face it, you are going to look at his body, and you are going to know he is dead. And as I thought this, the hope still hovered on the edge of my thoughts that there had been a mistake, and that it would not be Rudi when I got inside, but someone else. But it was a hope which I knew, even as I let it wash over me, was futile.

Someone turned the handles and swung the doors back. Besides everything else, there was also fear now. If it *were* Rudi, would he be physically all right? Had his head hit the dashboard and been cut? I had been told this hadn't happened, but the terror remained.

I had also been told by the doctor we had seen, who had been told by the ambulance driver, who had been told by the motorist who had called the ambulance, what had happened. Rudi had been in one of the Vanguard Security vans, waiting at a roundabout for a gap to appear in the traffic so that he could pull out. Suddenly, he had seemed to sit up in his seat as if he'd been hit with something very heavy from behind, and had clutched at his head. Then he had fallen forward, hitting the horn and setting it off. The motorist behind had pulled him out and telephoned 999. Rudi was dead by the time he arrived at the hospital.

The cause of death, said the doctor who told me all this, would not be known until an autopsy had been performed, but he suspected a haemorrhage in the brain. It did not leave any marks, he assured me, nor had Rudi hurt himself in his last moments. None the less, I was not assured, besides which I was also fearful of whatever expression I was going to find on Rudi's face.

Arthur and Vicki propelled me gently forward. I stepped across the threshold and found myself in a big room with lovely arched windows filled with coloured glass. I felt an immediate sense of relief that it wasn't a morgue, like in a film, with drawers for the bodies and a slab for the corpse. This was like a chapel. It was filled with blue and red light and suddenly I was glad I had come. It was going to be fine.

Another door opened, not the one through which we had come in, and a man wheeled a trolley forward. He parked it in the middle of the room. I went over and saw Rudi. There was a sheet around him, all the way round his body like a cocoon, and it came right up to his neck. There was another sheet on top which hung down at the sides.

I heard the others coming up and stopping a little way behind me as I stared at Rudi's face. He didn't look any different from the morning before when, half-dozing, I'd glanced at him on the pillow beside me.

'Yes, that's my husband,' I said this to the police detective who was with us.

I could feel Rudi there in the room, not quite in sight but close by me. However, with every second that was passing, he was fading, like a torch with a waning battery. This was our last time together. Goodbye, I thought, and the next instant I knew he had finally slipped from the room and was gone.

I stood stock-still for a while, not wanting to move, and then I heard my sister coughing. We all left together, none of us speaking, and we remained silent as we went through the hospital, the detective following behind at a discreet distance.

15

At the police station we were brought to an interview room and asked to wait. After a few minutes an inspector arrived, a different policeman from the one who had been in the hospital. He was carrying a brown carrier bag with an envelope Sellotaped to the side.

After he had introduced himself and sat down, he opened the envelope and tipped it sideways, spilling the contents on to the table. The first thing to tumble out was Rudi's East German wristwatch, with its brown leather strap which I had given him on our first Christmas together. This was followed by his wallet, also brown and battered, the stitching coming undone on one side, his Polish–English dictionary with its red cover, an ironed, unused handkerchief, a Lipsyl, its cracked case mended with a piece of plaster that was now grubby from his pocket, a packet of fuses, a pencil with a rubber, a biro, a collection of ten and twenty pence coins in the Midland Bank bag where he kept the loose change needed for parking meters, his black comb, and finally, his sunglasses.

'Would you like to see the clothes?' He indicated the bulging brown bag.

'I don't think my sister needs to,' said Vicki abruptly.

The inspector manoeuvred a book in front of me and asked if I would sign it.

'It's just a formality. So we can say you've had everything back.'

Looking about for a pen – I wasn't going to sign with Rudi's biro – that was when I remembered something forgotten for years. . . .

I am sitting at home, at the kitchen table. I am wearing my white socks and my patent-leather shoes. My mother is talking to my sister Vicki, explaining something important, judging by her tone of voice. She is not explaining it to me because I am thought to be too young to understand, which is why I am just left, sitting and listening.

'I am no longer Mrs Geoffrey Baring,' I hear my mother saying, 'I am Mrs Anne Maude Baring now,' and she continues, stressing over and over again that she is Anne Maude.

I have no understanding of the social niceties of the matter at the time – this came later – but I catch the drift. My father has gone away and as far as she is concerned, he is as good as dead . . .

From his pocket the inspector had produced a pen which I took. I wrote 'Mrs R. Janowski' and the date after my name, and then the receipt book was taken from me and closed.

16

Arthur was at the wheel. Vicki sat beside him. I was in the back of Arthur's car with Tiffany.

– Arthur drives and I am in the back From time to time I can feel the cat moving through the side of her wicker basket –

A device to freshen the air hung from the rear-view mirror. There was a pine tree painted on it but it didn't smell of pine. It had an antiseptic smell which reminded me of school lavatories on cold mornings.

– I look out through the window We are in Hounslow and to me it all looks newly built One great gust of wind, I think, and the whole lot would just blow away –

In the street there was a Belisha beacon flashing at a zebra crossing and school-children were crossing over, shouting and crowing. Further on we passed a parade of newish shops with their names up in plastic, and two girls eating ice-creams, their pink tongues licking the cones where the ice-cream had dribbled.

– We turn left I have a view of an industrial estate The factories are all low buildings, shaped like aircraft hangars, gated and fenced Now, more houses, semi-detached ones Fancy porches, bow windows, front paths of crazy paving – every householder has added some sort of embellishment but it doesn't make any difference of course   Underneath, every house is just a copy of every other one –

I stared out at another street. More shops. People again. Women in summer dresses, the first of the season, strolling in the pale sunshine and showing their white arms and legs. I felt myself growing angry. How dare these people enjoy the day, I thought. How dare they walk in the sun and eat ice-creams when I have lost the most important person in my life.

– These people remind me of bread, I think, with their thick thighs and pale skins, they remind me of bread which is white and damp and tasteless –

That was the last diary entry which wrote itself in my head. The words stopped rising then and were replaced by a feeling of disgust and anger and nausea, all mixed together.

I opened the manila envelope and pulled out Rudi's comb. There were a couple of his blond wispy hairs caught between the tines. I lifted the comb to my nose and I could smell him and his head, mixed up with the plastic of the comb. Tears started to roll down my cheeks as a feeling of poignancy and nostalgia for him overwhelmed me.

Suddenly, I was in the place of mists and whispers, where I had been the evening before. Rudi was there in the fog somewhere, and like a word on the tip of the tongue he was about to appear at any moment, if I could only just hold on . . .

Four

17

We were eating breakfast, late, when the telephone rang. My mother looked up from the other side of the table where she was spreading marmalade on a piece of toast. She had come up to stay with me the afternoon after Rudi died.

'It's the telephone, dear,' said my mum.

Rather than pick up the telephone on the sideboard, I went out to the other one in the hall. I act like this without thinking when my mother is with me.

It was the inspector, the one who had returned Rudi's possessions.

'I'm very sorry to trouble you,' he said politely.

There is a window in the hall beside the telephone which looks out on to an interior light-well, and my eyes ran to the bottom where I saw a pair of old tights, a Weetabix box and a deflated football.

'The post mortem has been completed,' said the inspector. 'This is off the record, but it seems it is most probable that your husband died of a haemorrhage of the brain.

'The point I'm ringing about, anyway, is that you can go ahead now with the funeral. When you decide on the undertakers, will you let me have their names so I can inform the hospital?'

Why wasn't there some benign agency, I wondered, to take this matter out of the hands of the relatives?

' . . . Are you there, Mrs Janowski?'

'Yes,' I said, 'I am.'

My eyes ran upwards until I was looking out the top of the shaft at a lid of grey sky.

'It's good to know I can look forward to speaking to you very soon then,' he said persuasively. 'Goodbye.'

I put down the phone and went back to the living-room. I sat down and put my hands on the table. My mum was watching me closely. The pain thumped away. I started to cry.

When I felt better again, I got myself dressed and went down to Mrs Small's. I pressed the bell and Mrs Small herself opened the door. She is short, with wiry black hair and fat arms.

'Oh,' said Mrs Small. She looked at me with a startled expression, then recovered quickly. 'I hear you had a bit of trouble,' she said in a manner that was gentle by her standards. 'I was very sorry to hear about your husband.'

Although she looked like the old Mrs Small – same dark eyes, same Claddagh ring on the same pudgy finger, same awful ski-pants – this was not the abrasive Mrs Small with whom I usually dealt but someone altogether mellower.

'I wonder,' I began, 'I can't find my Yellow Pages. Could I borrow yours?'

'Certainly, no trouble at all.'

Mrs Small waddled off down her hall, past the walls

lined with coaching horns, and disappeared into her living-room. I sniffed the familiar and unmistakable smell of the Smalls – a not unpleasant mixture of boiled clothes and bleach, mixed up with the atmosphere of hot rooms where the windows are never opened. Just inside their door there was an ugly teak sideboard, and on top lay a Bible, its black spine split and mended with Sellotape, which I had seen many Sunday mornings caught in the crook of Reg's arm as he set off for church with his wife. It was after I noticed it that the dog started yapping.

'Stop that!' I heard, 'and get in your basket.'

Mrs Small emerged from the living-room, hurried towards me and handed over the Yellow Pages.

'Here you are and I've slipped a little surprise inside for you.'

'Thank you.'

'It was actually your brother-in-law – is it Arthur? – who came,' she dropped her voice to a whisper, 'and told us, just last week, just after it happened. That was so good of him. We do need to know what's going on, you know.'

Mrs Small fixed on me with her small dark eyes and pushed out her considerable bust.

'You're very kind,' I said hypocritically.

I turned away and began to move across the courtyard.

'Don't forget, you can count on us,' Mrs Small called after me.

I heard her front door close.

On the stairs I fished out her gift from inside the flyleaf. It was a pamphlet and on the front I read:

'I am the Lord and I am the Resurrection,' said Jesus Christ

I started reading while my feet moved automatically up the stairs.

The gist of it was that if we could find God, all our questions would be answered. If we could find God, indwelling in our hearts and souls, then we would understand that everything that happened was part of His plan.

But how could a brain haemorrhage be part of God's plan, I wondered, especially since He was a God who was meant to love us? And why did He take away the people we loved? What could we or He possibly gain from that? And what could they, the dead, possibly gain from that? And then my memory drifted back to my last morning with Rudi . . . .

I am lying under the duvet asleep, warm and safe. Rudi is awake, his hand on my back, and he is pressing with his groin against me.

He whispers, 'Come on,' and rolls on to me. We make love and he comes while I am half-awake.

With his weight and his warmth and his hot breath on my skin, I start drifting back to sleep, that deep, lazy, early-morning sleep.

'Let's not go to work,' I say. 'Let's start the holiday today.'

He slowly pulls himself out of me and sits up. Then he takes his watch from the bedside table and begins to wind it.

'Better not,' he says, and I ask why.

'We socialists work harder, you know,' he says, as he liked to joke.

He brings me a cup of tea, and while I sip it he runs a bath. I hear him splashing around and singing. Then he comes back to the bedroom with his hair tousled and says, 'Bath,' and I reach out with my arms and he pulls me up from the bed . . .

Yet supposing we had decided to skip work, as we could have. It would have been a different day then, and who is to say that would have happened. He might have lived. That's the trouble with everything being according to a plan seen in advance. We don't have plans, at least people like us don't. We may be going along one way, but then on whim, or for some other reason, we can just change and go in completely the opposite direction. Our lives can turn on a pinhead.

God's plan, God's plan, I thought, there is no God's plan. There is just plain, stubborn, incomprehensible mess without any order. I tore the tract in half and stuffed it in my pocket.

18

From the list of funeral directors in the Yellow Pages I chose one in Goldhawk Road and dialled the number.

'Lambert's,' answered a cheerful male voice at the other end.

'The undertakers?'

'Certainly is.'

'I wanted to inquire about the cost of a funeral.'

'Hang on a moment, I'm going to hand you over to my wife. She deals with inquiries.'

The picture forming in my mind to go with the voice at the other end, was a big man with a red face who was always smiling, a sort of latter-day Laughing Cavalier.

'Yes?'

The new voice was nasal and feminine. Middle-aged, I imagined, and flat-chested, with bony hips which stuck out through her clothes.

'You wanted to inquire about the cost of a funeral. Is it a burial or a cremation?'

'I don't know.'

Mother had put herself on the arm of the arm-chair closest to the telephone and was giving me her

Oh-please-tell-me-what's-going-on-look, while holding her head sideways to catch what was coming out of the receiver. 'Ask about a burial,' she whispered loudly, and I glowered back at her.

'I want to inquire about a cremation,' I said, opening the notepad I had and holding my pencil ready.

'Are you a relative?'

'I'm the widow.'

'Was the death natural, or were there other causes? I have to ask this because it's got a bearing on our prices. An unnatural death and a cremation, you see, work out a bit cheaper than a natural death.'

'I see,' I said, not having the slightest idea what she was talking about. 'It was an unnatural death, a haemorrhage.'

'Could you give me some idea as to what you have it in mind to spend?'

I said, 'I've never done this before.'

'I see. Well, I'll begin with our starting prices and we can work our way up from there. Right, at the very bottom we're talking seven hundred and twenty-one pounds with a following car, six hundred and ninety-eight pounds without one, that's for the cremation. It would be more, as I said, if we had to have the two cremation certificates, but as it's an unnatural we don't need them. That'll save forty-seven pounds, which is something anyway.'

'Seven hundred and twenty-one pounds?' I said disbelievingly.

'That's right. That's the cheapest. Removal from the hospital or mortuary, that's forty-two pounds. Minister's fee, twenty-one pounds. Gratuity of nine pounds to the mortuary attendant when we collect, and another nine pounds to the crematorium attendant. Cremation fee, seventy-five pounds. For that they will also scatter the ashes for you in the Garden of Remembrance. That makes one hundred and fifty-six pounds.'

'But you say seven hundred and twenty-one pounds . . .'

'Hold on. On top of these costs, we now have our five hundred and sixty-five pounds. That covers the cost of embalming, the viewing of the remains in the Chapel of Rest, one hearse and one following car. Total, seven hundred and twenty-one pounds if you add it up, and on top of that there's VAT. But that's nothing to do with us, that's the government, isn't it?'

My mum had taken the pad on which I had scribbled down the figures, and as she now stared at them she shook her head.

'Do you want to take the ashes away or do you want them scattered?'

'I don't know.'

'If you want to take them away for private disposal you can do that, but it'll be a further five pounds for a polyurn.'

'A polyurn, five pounds,' I hissed to my mum and she added it to the other figures.

'Will the ashes go abroad?'

I hadn't thought, but it was just conceivable they might go to Poland.

'Maybe.'

'In that case, you'll need a certificate which'll be a further three pounds.'

'Certificate, three pounds,' I called out.

'Are the remains in London?'

'The West Middlesex Hospital.'

'That's out near Heathrow, isn't it? If it's over twenty miles from here there might be a slight increase in the removal costs, but hold on. Maurice, Maurice,' she called. There was a good deal of indistinct shouting and then she returned.

'It is more than twenty miles, my husband tells me, but we count it as less than twenty miles all the same. Now, what name?'

'I was going to try some other numbers,' I said feebly.

'Then let me take a note of your name. That way, if you ring back, I'll know who you are.'

'Mrs Alibi,' I said without hesitation.

'A-l-i-b-i?'

'Yes'

'Goodbye.'

19

The second undertaker gave me about the same price and so did the third and the fourth. I asked the fifth undertaker whether I could bring Rudi's body to the crematorium myself – this would have reduced the costs to about a hundred pounds – and he laughed.

'Oh no, that wouldn't be possible. You'd have to buy a coffin yourself, you see,' he said, 'and you'll find no undertaker would sell you one. We don't sell to the man on the street just like that. Besides, there are also innumerable matters of certification which members of the general public aren't able to deal with.'

Innumerable matters of certification! He went by the extraordinary name of Henderpen and I pictured him as having a tiny body and a huge head, thin lips, and long fingernails with dirt under them.

'I'm afraid you have to face facts,' he said. 'It's six hundred and ninety-nine pounds plus VAT without a following car and that's the minimum we can do it for.'

It was a racket in short – you had to use them and you had to pay for them and there was no way round it.

I put the telephone down and I stared at the figures jotted down on the pad.

'Of course, there won't just be these costs, will there?' Mother said. 'There'll be flowers. You'll obviously want to bring people back here. You might need something to wear. We'll have to tip the undertakers. VAT. We're talking more than a thousand, aren't we?'

Where was I going to get that amount of money, I thought, and on top of that there were the bills, I remembered. I had found them in the blue file in the sideboard where Rudi had kept all our paperwork. Why, I do not know, but he had not paid anything in the months before he died. The day I made the discovery, starting to leaf through them, my hands had shaken and my stomach had knotted. You won't get anywhere fretting about these now, I had thought, and I'd stuffed the bills back in the file where I had found them, and I did the same again now by pushing all thought about the cost of the funeral out of my mind.

'Money, money, money,' my mum said, 'it's all anybody wants,' and she continued, 'I won't be able to help you much.'

Her lined face with its brown eyes, magnified behind her spectacle lenses, hovered in front of me.

'Maybe Vicki and Arthur can help, but I think it's tight for them with the children. Have you anything in the bank?'

I shook my head. Rudi and I had never been ones for saving, I said.

'What are you going to do, then?' my mother asked.

'I don't know. I suppose we'd better go for the cheapest.'

This, it turned out, was Henderpen's, and I wasn't going to give my business there, so I rang Lambert's who were the next best.

'Mrs Alibi, isn't it? Recognize the voice,' Mr Lambert said, when he picked up the phone.

'No, Janowski . . .' I replied brazenly.

After I had finished giving him the details and put down the telephone, my mother said, 'I'm sure something will turn up, you know. It always does.'

She didn't sound very convincing.

Five

20

It was Monday, midday. I looked at myself in my freckled wardrobe mirror. I was wearing a straight black skirt to the knee, a white blouse with pleated front, my black jacket with its square silver buttons, black stockings and black flat suede shoes. I didn't look bad, I thought, and Rudi would be proud of me. He liked when I dressed up, saying it made up for the dreariness of his life in Poland.

I went through to the living-room. Vicki and Arthur sat side by side on the sofa. Arthur's suit was a battleship-grey colour. It was trim and elegant and yet he looked deeply uncomfortable in it. Vicki was wearing her black coat, buttoned right up to her neck, and her hair was pinned high on top of her head. And as she was sitting so very straight, she looked very dramatic.

'Let's go,' said my mother.

We left thinking we were going to be late, but in the event, when we pulled up to the crematorium gate, the man in the little hut beside it said, 'You're early.'

From my seat in the back of Arthur's car I looked past him into the hut. His lunch was laid out on a card-table

– a tomato in quarters, slices of buttered bread, and a thermos with steaming tea.

'You can wait in the car park outside the chapel. Follow the road along,' he said.

Arthur drove off slowly. The road was blue and curved through lawns strewn with cut grass, and past a row of poplar trees on which a few early leaves just showed. A huge graveyard appeared then, stretching away to our left. I could see headstones and crypts, tombs and crosses, all jumbled together, and looking like a model city of skyscrapers.

So the day had come at last, I thought, the final, technical ending. I slipped a finger inside my handbag and checked I had brought a handkerchief, and at the same moment I started to cry.

The crematorium was a stone building, black from a hundred years of London dirt. Painters' boards and scaffolding were piled outside. The interior was cold and smelt of turpentine and had newly painted fern-green walls.

The minister was old. 'I'm afraid I didn't have the pleasure of knowing the deceased,' he began, in a cracked and wavering voice. I had agreed to a Christian service and now I regretted it and felt angry that I had let my mother and Arthur organize everything. From this mood I slipped into a sort of trance pretty soon during which I heard only odd phrases from the minister about the peacefulness of death, the bountifulness of God's mercy, and so on. The minister finished with a few words in Polish. He'd learnt them off by heart and he spoke them so slowly that it was painful to listen to him.

Then the conveyor-belt started up and the whole place was filled with the echoing sound of the electric motor which powered it. I watched the coffin trundle away until its end was nudging the curtain. I wanted to utter a terrible cry, to rush forward and clasp the end and stop it disappearing. Yet I was rooted to the spot and did not move, let alone cry out, but watched silently as the brown curtain lifted and the coffin slowly glided on until it was all the way through and then the curtain dropped again and it was gone. The next moment the conveyor belt stopped and there was an eerie stillness with only the sound of the congregation breathing. Behind the curtain, I thought, they are getting it ready for the furnace. That was when one of the undertakers opened the side door and a square of brilliant sunlight fell on the red tile floor of the crematorium. There was a sturdy grip on each elbow and I let myself be guided forward.

Outside we waited for the remains which, when they appeared, came in a small brown cardboard box, which weighed about the same as a pair of new shoes.

21

The tea was laid out on the table in the living-room. There were cup cakes already prised out of their foil holders, a jam roll sprinkled with caster sugar, an Irish barm brack and sandwiches – egg-and-cress, egg-and-cucumber, egg-and-tomato. My mum had made them before the cremation and had left them under a damp tea-towel to keep them moist.

'I could eat a horse,' said Arthur from the table, and Vicki opposite him shook her head and said, 'Nothing ever interferes with your appetite, does it?'

Rudi's old uncle from Wembley was sitting on the sofa, nervously running his hand round and round the inside of his homburg while talking to Zeeta. Pam and her husband stood in front of the fireplace. She wore a double-breasted dress and he was in a double-breasted jacket. Sarah sat on the other armchair, frowning as she rolled a cigarette and talking to Ron who was standing beside her. As she was about to lick the gummed edge, she looked up at me and smiled. Three of Rudi's workmates were in the corner in a tight, silent knot, a little embarrassed because they didn't know anyone. I was standing with two half-empty wine bottles. I was just thinking, I must talk to them, when I heard Arthur whispering to my mother who was refilling his teacup, 'What was the damage this afternoon?' and saw my mother mouthing, 'A thousand,' and then saw Vicki glowering at my mother and shaking her head and whispering, 'Arthur, you are so tactless.'

Talking to Rudi's workmates a few moments later, I started to cry. Everyone and everything seemed so absurd. My mother took the wine bottles and gave me her handkerchief and I wiped my face. It smelt of her cold cream and her scent and the lace around the edges was rough on my skin.

She buttered a piece of brack on both sides, led me over to the table and sat me down in front of it.

'You liked it like this as a child, do you remember?' she whispered.

The pain felt like a hot rock in the middle of my body. It had squashed out every organ and it occupied the whole space.

'We'll do something, we'll find the money, don't worry,' Arthur whispered. He didn't understand.

'We will,' agreed Vicki. Nor did my sister.

Her face was flushed. Wisps of her hair had come undone from the pile on top of her head and were stuck to her hot skin. She unbuttoned her coat and Arthur helped her to take it off. She was wearing a plain blue dress underneath.

'How about a nice cup of tea,' my mother said, poured the cup out and set it in front of me.

Six

22

One day my father was at home with us and the next he was gone. His absence was like having a stone in my shoe. I had to walk on it and walk on it and walk on it until my foot was raw. I bore it well and nobody knew, only Vicki . . .

It was the summer and it was some time after my dad had left. It was the middle of the day. Vicki and I were in our straw boaters and our cotton dresses. Our white socks were pulled up to our knees. Our leather shoes were polished. The bows at the back of our dresses were properly tied. We were on the promenade by the sea. The Channel was grey and green. There must have been ships floating on it and the shingle must have whispered as the surf carried it backwards and forwards. I can't remember why my mum wasn't with us. It was unlike her to let us out alone at that age.

We turned away from the sea and into a street. A row of South Coast houses stared down at us. They were old and crooked and made of flint and brick. The holes behind the boot-scrapers beside each doorway were like the dark beady eyes of an insect.

We walked on without speaking. There was a smell of fish and seaweed and salt. We got further from the coast and this faded and the smell of the town grew stronger. The odour was a mixture of gas and cabbage and burnt Yorkshire pudding. There was also the thin but sweet smell of candy floss that carried all the way from the arcades on the front.

On the far side of town lay The Eagle public house, a big square building which looked like a toad, crouching and waiting to spring, and which smelt of beer.

We stopped before the double doors in front. The doors with their worn brass handplates looked back at us. The windows on either side looked back as well. The glass in the windows was the kind you couldn't see through. It kept out the prying eyes of wives and children. The Eagle was where our dad used to drink.

Now we had got there we didn't know what to do. We didn't dare go in and we didn't dare turn back. So we just stood and waited for something to happen.

Men went in and men came out. Some looked at us and hurried on. Some slowed down and gave us a wink or a little drunken wave. One gave us threepence each and told us to enjoy ourselves in the arcades.

Still we did not move. The threepenny pieces grew hot in our hands. Each time we switched the coins from one palm to the other, we smelt the brassy smell of money and sweat.

Suddenly our dad came out. I recognized the hair plastered with Brylcreem. He combed it so flat, it was almost like a bathing cap. I recognized the pointed nose. I recognized the intense brown eyes. I have the same eyes.

He was wearing labouring clothes, an old jacket and no tie. His trousers were held up with a thick leather belt which we could see under his jacket. A bit of the trousers fanned out over the top of the belt. He had lost a lot of weight. If I saw him now, I'd see a man worn with cares, but I wasn't able to see that then.

Dad looked at us. Two other men who were labouring on the site where he was working had come out with him and they were looking at us as well. He said something to them. How the hell did they get here, was probably what he was thinking.

He started looking odd, even angry, and I could remember him looking angry from when he lived with us. I also remember how surprised I was. I had assumed he'd be pleased to see us, but then I didn't know anything at that age.

I looked at his face. I saw his pointed nose, his dull blond hair, his blond eyebrows. He was looking at us without blinking. We asked him would he like to come home. He shook his head and laughed.

We said, 'Will you come to the house? Just come once, for tea. Just come over for a minute and play with us in the garden, and if you don't like the garden you can play with us in our bedroom. We have a new doll's house.'

He shook his head and laughed. His colleagues mumbled and shook their heads and talked pointedly about the time. He lit a cigarette.

Suddenly Vicki and I got clever. 'Come to the Dark House,' we said, 'where we play. We'll show you our spells and our magic place in the middle of the big green bush and the ballroom and the cupboard full of musical instruments, and we'll be alone.'

He agreed. Our hearts soared. We ran home in high spirits. We said nothing to my mother. I can't remember if we slept. I doubt it.

The place we called the Dark House was a Victorian mansion. The old owner had made a lot of money in hats. After he died it had been locked up and left untouched and unvisited for years, and that's how we found it.

Upstairs there were double beds and rotting bolsters, wardrobes filled with top hats and frock-coats, and cane bustles.

At the end of the numerous corridors there were lavatories filled with brown water. We found a swollen rat drowned in one once and after that we didn't go in the closets any more.

Downstairs, there were rooms filled with mildewed furniture, and a ballroom. Under the small stage there was a cupboard filled with mouldering violins and cellos. There was also a piano. It still played, although out of key.

The kitchens were filled with copper pans which had gone green with age, and cooking utensils which Vicki and I could never work out a use for. Further on were the pantries and sculleries, and musty corridors. Everywhere the plaster was peeling off the walls. The tackrooms lay beyond. These still had old saddles rotting in them, and riding hats which shed their velvet when we touched them. Without their coverings they were like bald heads.

Outside, behind the offices, were the greenhouses. The glass in these was all slimy-green and the frames were sagging. Finally, there was the kitchen garden. It was completely overgrown with trees, shrubs and a forest of rhododendron bushes. In the middle of these we made our camp. It was dark and green and a place of magic.

The next morning, as soon as we had finished breakfast, we were off.

We went to the orchard wall at the back of the Dark House. It had tumbled down and was easy to climb. This was where we had agreed to meet our dad.

We waited and waited but he never came, and so there was only one way now to turn – to magic.

From the walls of the scullery we collected lumps of red-coloured plaster and then, using an ancient mortar and pestle, we ground the plaster into a fine dust.

In the yard we worked the pump. The handle was flaky with rust and the water was a long way down. I got very hot and tired as I moved the handle up and down, and my hands went red from the iron. When the water eventually gushed, we caught it in a jam-jar.

In the middle of the dark rhododendron bush we mixed the water with the plaster to a paste, and then carved intricate patterns in the ground with specially pointed sticks. These we filled with our plaster mush. Then we stood in the middle of our magic inscriptions and recited our magic words. We were solemn, did not smile and did not laugh either.

Our magic had worked wonders in the past. I had wished for a red yo-yo and it had brought me one. I had wished for a yellow straw boater with a blue ribbon and it had brought me one. I had wished for a small black clip-purse to keep my coppers in and it had brought me one. Now it was going to bring us our dad.

We finished and headed back towards the orchard

wall. We had no doubt we'd find Dad waiting, sitting on the tumbled-down bricks and smoking a cigarette. But when we arrived we found he wasn't there. We looked around. He wasn't waiting anywhere.

So be it, we said, and shrugged. Our powers of recovery were sensational. So he hadn't come. Well, we'd have to go for stronger magic, that was all.

The next day we mixed a new potion, using red and yellow plaster this time. We didn't any longer want to bring him to the orchard wall. We'd learnt our lesson. We wanted to find him instead. What we wanted was the name of the village where he was labouring.

We stripped down to our knickers and painted ourselves with the mush and danced slowly. Out of the blue we both picked Oakhampton. It was a village a couple of miles from where we lived. We washed off the mush with pump water and headed there straight away.

When we arrived we went to the Post Office to inquire about our dad.

'Oh yes,' said the woman behind the counter. 'There were men working here and your father was with them, yes. Only they're gone now,' she added.

We walked home. We were ecstactic. We were desolate. The magic had worked. We'd gone to the right place. The magic had failed. We had missed him.

Day three. We made a paste of red and yellow and green plaster. We daubed our naked bodies *and* we made our magic patterns on the floor. We chanted our spells *and* we danced at the same time. We were more solemn than ever. We took longer than ever.

We finished and we dressed. We went to The Eagle. Our aims were more modest now. Just to catch him as he came out with his cronies. Just to talk to him. We were only eight and six but already the lesson was sinking in. Never expect too much. Never get promises, especially from those you love. Take what you get and ask for nothing more.

It was lunchtime when we arrived. There was the same smell of stale beer as before.

We stood before the double doors. I straightened my straw boater. I pulled my white socks up. I pushed my hair behind my ears.

We walked in. We could only do that because we were together. The men around the tables looked up from their glasses and their dominoes. I can still remember their expressions to this day. They were absolutely astonished. Two little girls had walked in where little girls never went.

'We're looking for our dad,' we said to the landlord. We gave his name – Geoffrey. We gave the surname – Baring.

One or two men sitting along the counter nodded. Once this had been Geoffrey Baring's local, they mumbled, but not for a long time, they said.

But then, just the other day, hadn't he come in for a pint? said someone.

Been in the area, hadn't he? said someone else. Hadn't been in for ages before that though, had he?

That was right. He'd moved away. Trouble with the missus. Couldn't hit it off with her.

'No sign of him, girls, sorry,' the landlord said to us.

He was sad because he wasn't able to say to us what we wanted to hear. He liked to please children. He was also impatient. We were under-age. He could be reported and he wanted us out. He wanted to do it nicely though.

We looked at him. I looked at him. Don't you see how sad I am? my expression said. Don't you want to help me? Don't you want to help us find our dad?

'Go on now. Go home to your mother. This isn't a place for children,' the landlord said.

We went down to the sea and stood on the hard shingle beach. The Channel was grey and still and almost looked solid enough to walk on, and if it had been we would have, and kept going until France.

Staring at the Channel, I recognized for the first time in my life I had been defeated. I had wanted something very badly but events were simply beyond our control. What I couldn't understand was why. Why couldn't a child see her father?

I thought about it and then I had the glimmering of an understanding. It might be right that we ought to see our dad but that wasn't a reason why it *should* happen. Sometimes what was right didn't happen and you just had to live with it. That was the way life was.

I only ever saw my father once more. It was at the time I was in Beirut. I was home on my holidays and I had gone to Haslemere for some reason I have now forgotton.

I went to the bus depot and got on to a bus parked there. There was a man stretched out asleep on the bench seat right in front of the door. The blond hair was grey. The pointed nose was red and had veins in the side. The cheeks were swollen and wrinkled. He was in a grubby conductor's uniform and the ticket machine was beside him.

For a long time I stood and looked at him. He was

snoring quietly. I wondered whether to wake him or not and in the end I decided I didn't want to. I didn't want him to open his eyes and discover me there, just like that, looking down on him as he lay stretched out in his dirty uniform. Nor did I want him to discover I had seen him while he had been asleep.

I slipped away and hopped on the first bus leaving the depot, anxious to get away. The bus brought me to a town nearby, from where I made my way home. I never went back to Haslemere again.

My dad was killed in the end. In the garage where I'd found him, a driver reversed carelessly and crushed him against a pillar. I was back in Beirut by this time and my mother wrote and told me about it, enclosing a clipping from the local Haslemere paper. She didn't go to the funeral and to this day I don't even know where the grave is.

23

Rudi and I tried to have a child for three years. We did all the things you have to do and we did them at the right time of the month. But nothing happened and then Rudi died.

The day after the funeral I noticed my period was late. I could not believe it at first. I did some calculations with the diary and found that, definitely, I was overdue.

I went to the bathroom and took the Calculator out of the cabinet. I'd bought it years before, when we'd made the decision to try for a child. It resembled those things which amateur photographers of my dad's generation used, except that instead of calculating F-stops and depth of field, it worked out the time of conception and birthdate.

I sat down on the side of the bath and I calculated how long I was overdue and from that worked backwards. I stared at the date at the end of the arrow. It fell within a fertile period. Had we made love that night? I asked myself.

We had, I remembered. That was the night we'd been out to eat in the Zeus Kebab House. It's in a terrace house in a street off the Harrow Road. The kitchen is in the front room and there are four tables crowded into the back-room The walls are covered with family photographs, fishing nets and cork floats. It was one of our favourite places. We drank a good bit and as soon as we got into bed we fell on one another.

Sitting in the bathroom, I decided I must be pregnant.

I didn't tell my mother. I told no one. I just went out alone and bought one of those Predictor kits.

That same evening I was sitting by the window in my living-room. I was looking out at the Westway. Mother was knitting behind me. It was dusk and I was watching the shining headlamps of the cars streaming out of London.

I was brooding about the Chapel of Rest. What I couldn't get out of my mind about my time in the light-filled, peaceful room, was the overwhelming sense I had had that Rudi had been in there with me. Aha, I now thought, Rudi knew, that's why he was there. It was so important that what we had been trying to achieve over all those years had finally been achieved, he had had to come and see me.

When I had come out of the chapel I had felt dazed and numb. I had also felt full, I remembered, and now that made sense to me. What I couldn't understand was how I'd missed these signs at the time.

I reached out and touched the wooden window-ledge. Please let him be all right, I prayed. Automatically, I assumed it was a he. Rudi's child would have to be a boy, wouldn't it? I woke up the next morning and did the test. Negative. I couldn't believe it. I did it again. Same story. I checked the sell-by date. It was well within it. Well, something else was the matter with it then. I couldn't trust it. I knew I was pregnant. I knew.

I went off to the Health Centre. My doctor is an Australian, called Dr Swift. The walls of his surgery are covered with drawings by his children of rockets and monsters and rainbows. He is a young doctor. He has a beard and is plump.

'Hello,' he said, when I came through his door. He gave me a broad smile. 'I was so pleased when I saw your name on the list of patients this morning. I was going to ring you. I've got some good news.'

I sat down and I said, 'I have some news as well. What's yours?'

'The National Health moves slowly but it does move. I have an appointment for yourself and your husband at the clinic next month. Let's see. I saw you two in February,' he said, picking up my record card, 'and the appointment is for May. Three months' wait isn't bad, you know.'

'Rudi died,' I said bluntly.

He looked incredulous. I told him everything.

'I can't believe it,' he said, when I had finished, 'I can't . . . And I'm so sorry I didn't know. If I had I wouldn't have put my foot in it like that . . .'

'I think I might be pregnant,' I said.

He looked at me in a way I'd never seen him look before. It was what I'd call odd, sceptical, uncomfortable.

'Have you done a test?' he asked.

Since the Predictor kit obviously wasn't working properly, it was as if I hadn't, I had decided . . .

'No, I haven't,' I said.

I brought my early morning urine to him the next morning. That was Thursday. He told me the results would be due the next morning and I thought, Rudi will have been a fortnight dead then.

For the next twenty-four hours I kept thinking, I'm pregnant, and when I was out I continuously played little games with myself.

If I didn't see the colour blue in the street before I counted a hundred, it was a girl. If, by the time I reached the Belisha beacon on Westbourne Grove, the green man had started to flash, it was a boy. If turnips in the greengrocer's were on sale for a figure which divided by three, it was twins.

I was suddenly extraordinarily careful in everything I did. Especially crossing the road and climbing up the stairs in a bus. Something precious was in me and I had to make certain nothing happened to it.

I woke up and it was Friday morning. It was just getting light. I could hear trains shunting on the sidings outside Paddington.

I fell asleep again and my mum called me later. I still hadn't told her or anyone. The knowledge was my secret treasure.

I was in the waiting-room in the Health Centre well before nine. Dr Swift passed through and I waved to him.

'Good morning,' he said. The way he spoke didn't say anything to me. It didn't say, Yes, you're pregnant, and it didn't say, No, you're not pregnant.

I read an article by a well-known actress: 'The Joys of Motherhood over Forty'. Then the buzzer sounded and the receptionist told me to go through.

Dr Swift was sitting behind his desk. There was a pile of manila files at his elbow.

He said, 'I'm sorry.' He sounded it. He shook his head.

'I shouldn't do this,' he said, and wrote me out a prescription. Something to help me to sleep at night and something to gee me up again in the morning.

I just said, 'Thank you,' and took it.

Out in the street I immediately threw the prescription away. Then I thought better of it. I went back to the litter-bin to retrieve it but the crumpled piece of paper had somehow managed to fall through the rubbish to the bottom. Passers-by stared at me as I pulled everything out but I didn't care. I had lost my father. I had lost my husband. I had lost my child. At least I wasn't going to lose my tablets.

I went to the Blue Sky and cried and cried and cried. George the waiter knew where I lived and he went and found Mum and she came and fetched me home.

24

My mother made Sunday lunch. We had roast beef and Yorkshire pudding, brussels sprouts and peas. Vicki and Arthur came with the twins, Cherry and Amanda.

The Wizard of Oz was on television that afternoon and we all watched it together. As the storm howled and Dorothy hurtled through the air, I remembered sitting in the same room, watching the same scene, only instead of my family I was with Rudi. This was not long after we had started living together.

'This is so bizarre,' he had kept saying throughout the film, 'this is so bizarre.'

It was a word which had just entered his vocabulary and he was keen to use it at every opportunity.

Needless to say, remembering this, I started crying.

Cherry and Amanda were sitting on the floor. They didn't look round or say anything but from the way their backs seemed to ripple beneath their ironed cotton dresses, I could sense their embarrassment. They were only thirteen. They were awkward. They were uncomfortable with their auntie crying.

I felt Vicki beside me on the sofa taking my hand and squeezing it. For a moment I felt vaguely resentful. It was easy to make such a gesture in her position. She had the husband. She had the family.

I didn't mind the twins' awkwardness. It was her having them that I kicked against, and my not having children.

'I don't know what's the matter with me,' I said untruthfully, but I knew perfectly well.

It was widowhood mixed up with the pain of discovering I wasn't pregnant which I was feeling. I imagined they guessed that, because I had told them everything. I might even have talked more about not being pregnant than I had about Rudi's death.

'This was one of my favourite films as a child,' I said. 'Remember, Mum, how much I wanted a dress like Judy Garland's?'

'I don't remember that at all,' she said, 'but then, most likely you didn't tell me.'

Her words trailed away. On the Yellowbrick Road, Dorothy and the Lion and the Tin Man trudged along. I no longer heard what was coming out of the television and inside my head everything was swirling.

It was late afternoon. We were sitting at the table drinking tea. My mother was walking round the room checking she hadn't left anything as well as searching for something.

'I can't find my hairbrush,' she said finally.

'I put it in your bag.'

Later when we were in the hall where there was no one to overhear us, she said, 'Are you sure you don't mind me going? I don't have to go now, you know.'

'I'll be all right,' I said, 'I'll be fine.'

In fact I couldn't wait for her to leave. I didn't want

to have to answer her questions any more, or to have to dredge around for words to explain how I felt to her. I found her sympathy suffocating. At the same time I was dreading being alone.

'If anything happens, I can always ring you, or go over to Vicki's or to Zeeta's,' I said.

I looked at her floating, shrivelled face. She would have stayed. I could tell that. I could also tell she was relieved. She didn't like being away from her things or her routine and London made her nervous. She was glad to be going home to what she knew.

At half-past six Arthur and Vicki took her off to catch her train. After they closed the front door behind them, I heard their footfalls as they all went down the stairs, and I was alone in the flat for the first time since Rudi died.

Then silence.

There was nothing to do, nothing. Not even the washing-up. The twins had done it, thinking it would be helpful. I sat down at the table and stared out of the window at the roofs below. I did not move. Suddenly I realized it was dark outside. I looked at my watch and I realized I'd been sitting there for hours.

Thank God I was going back to work.

I had a bath, shaved my legs and painted my nails. I felt distinctly anxious. I was perspiring. I went into my bedroom and looked at my bed. The sight of it increased my anxiety and made my heart beat faster.

I can't sleep in that, I thought. It represented us, Rudi and I. It was the quintessence of our marriage. It was also where we had failed to make our child.

With my mum in the flat, it had somehow been all

131

right sleeping in it, but now she had gone, it was different.

I made up the sofa-bed in the living-room. I used the sheets Mother had slept on and fell alseep with the smell of her cold cream and her coal tar soap all around me. It was a long, deep sleep I had, Whatever I dreamt, I never remembered it.

The next morning I was at the bus stop before eight. While I was waiting a man came up and asked me to sleep with him. He thought I was a prostitute. He showed me his wage-packet as proof he had money. He was an Indian or a Pakistani. Indignantly, I told him to go away, and he went off very quickly.

When I arrived at work Dolores was already in. She's Spanish and lisps and does the repairs. She keeps a prayer-book in her handbag and goes to Mass at seven every day. She was in one of her usual black dresses, sewing away, her face set in its usual expression.

She looked up when she saw me at the door, and when I came in she got up and kissed me.

Mr Sammi arrived next. He's a small, dapper man, less than five foot tall, with beautiful crinkly hair. He's never without the white stick of a Senior Service cigarette clamped between his nicotine-stained fingers. He found me at my desk opening the letters. He looked at me and smiled understandingly.

Next to roll in was Mabel with a present for me of some small sweet red tomatoes from her greenhouse. Mabel serves the customers. Her body is huge and heavy and she wears her fine white hair in a net decorated with pearls. 'I won't stand no nonsense' is her catch-phrase. If any of the temporary girls slip up

132

when Mabel's around, woe betide. She makes their lives a misery.

Last in was Eric. He clapped me on the back when he saw me. Eric drives the van and is a Heavy Metal fan. He's got an odd stare and long black hair. He's overweight and a white wedge of his stomach is always on show between his tee-shirt and his jeans.

Arthur had paid a visit, I discovered, and told them all what had happened.

At lunchtime Mr Sammi and I were alone in the office at the rear. He cleared his throat and asked me if I was all right. He offered me a further two weeks off, with full wages of course.

'Give you a chance to get yourself organized,' he said. Mr Sammi can be nice like that.

'Thank you, but I couldn't. I want to work, Mr Sammi. I want to keep my mind occupied. I don't want to sit at home and brood. Coming in here every day is the best possible thing I could do.'

He looked relieved. He'd made the offer. He'd done the right thing. Now the matter was closed.

The special treatment from the others went on for a couple of days but by the end of the week it was over. After that they talked to me the same way they always had. I was grateful for that. It was what I wanted, just being one of the gang again.

SUMMER

Seven

25

About six weeks after I went back to work, I learnt the date of the hearing at the coroner's court. I wanted to go and my mum suggested she come and stay and see me through it, and I agreed.

It was a Saturday afternoon when I went to Waterloo to meet her. Reaching the announcement board where I had gone to see at which platform her train would arrive, I found she was already sitting waiting on a bench.

'Hello, Mum,' I said.

She turned. Her eyes are brown, like mine, her mouth is small, unlike mine – I have my father's mouth – and there are lines on her forehead and running down from her nose.

'My dear,' she said.

By the clock in the middle of the board I saw I was forty minutes late, but Mum was making a brave effort not to show it. She put her arms around me and I felt her thin wrists pressing on my back. Still she didn't say a word and I knew that she wouldn't either.

'I'm sorry I'm late,' I said, releasing myself from her embrace and waggling my wrist to show I wasn't wearing my watch. The fact was, I'd woken up late and hung-over, and not wanting to make myself anxious on the journey, I'd deliberately left my watch at home.

'Not to worry,' she said generously, shaking her head and tossing her hair. She was wearing little black earrings, and on the collar of her khaki jacket she had sewn two small black squares.

Her suitcase when I picked it up was surprisingly light, as it always has been since we went on holidays as children. My luggage when I was a child, on the other hand, was always too heavy, and it seems to have gone on like this for the rest of my life. When I worked abroad it was a standing joke with Zeeta and the others that I was always the one with excess weight at the airport, and now I never seemed to have less than a full handbag and a carrier bag.

My mum was thirsty and I took her to a stall where the men behind the counter wore straw hats and striped aprons. We ordered two filter coffees and two glasses of water. The water tasted vaguely of chlorine. The coffee was strong and made my heart race. It reminded me of cocaine which a boyfriend in Beirut had sometimes given me. He was an oldish man and we used to go away for weekends to a little rose-coloured villa in the hills. I tried to recall his name but it was gone.

This is awful, I thought, waiting for Mum who was drinking her coffee in small, parsimonious sips. I was becoming like one of those old people I knew when I was young. They could remember Queen Victoria's Jubilee, the sinking of the *Titanic*, and the day the Great War ended, but they couldn't remember where they lived, what they'd had for lunch, or who they were.

I started watching the crowds and picked out a strong-looking man in his fifties, whose Brylcreemed hair lay flat on his scalp the same way my dad had worn his. The man had a companion, an Asian, about nineteen or twenty years old, and wearing baggy trousers.

'That wasn't a bad bit of grub,' said the older man, patting his stomach as they passed.

'I've finished,' said my mum. 'Shall we be going?' and we set off again.

The two men were in front of us and there was a white girl with them now. At the top of the steps leading down to the underground the Asian embraced her while the older one looked on. For the first time since Rudi died I thought about what it would be like to be held and I thought I would like it.

My mother was at the top of the steps and starting her descent. As I followed after her a great rush of hot air came up from the underground below and my eyes smarted and watered from the heat.

26

In the courtyard of Westbourne Mansions Mrs Small's dog started yapping as we passed her flat, and he didn't let up until we were on the turn half-way up the stairs, where we stopped for my mum to catch her breath.

'Bloody dog,' I said.

Mum's wrinkled hand lay on the banister rail. She still wears her gold wedding ring though she never saw my dad again after he left. The ring is loose around the bony finger but the slack skin of the joint prevents it falling off.

Some one in the courtyard began whistling and Mrs Small's dog started up again.

'I think it's cruel keeping an animal in the city,' said my mum, and we resumed climbing in silence.

My living-room was a mess. Saucers filled with cigarette butts everywhere, beside old glasses and dirty cereal bowls, newspapers and old cigarette packets. I hadn't washed or cleaned up all week, just come home each evening with wine and a take-away, got myself merry and fallen on to the sofa-bed where I'd been sleeping since my mum's last visit, and which stood unmade at the side of the room, the bedding all tangled on top of it.

Tut, tut, tut, I could hear Mum saying in her head as she looked around. Then she turned on her heel, went out to the kitchen and came back with a tray, and began piling it with ashtrays, bowls and glasses.

'Why don't you put away the bed, darling?' she said.

'Can't I leave it? You'll be sleeping on it later, won't you?'

'I don't think that would be very nice, do you, Cathy, sitting in a room all evening with a bed?'

I took the duvet wearily, caught the middle under my chin and folded it in half.

In the early evening I watched *The Price is Right* on television. When a fat lady contestant won a fridge-freezer, she jumped up in the air and two of her buttons popped off.

My mum made a salad for supper. There was beetroot in the middle of the plate and the juice stained the lettuce and the egg red.

'Have some bread, dear,' she said, offering the bread-board with the slices – so like her, this – already cut and buttered, two for me and two for her.

'I think a salad is a very settling thing, don't you?' she said.

She had a piece of egg on her fork. She dipped it into the little pile of salt on the side of her plate and then put it into her mouth.

'Bouillon is good as well. So are light soufflés. So is consommé.'

'Good for what?'

'When you're trying to get over something. But I don't think you can beat a nice, healthy salad. Crisp, fresh, green things, they have a wonderful effect. They clean out the tummy and they lift the spirits.'

She tapped the side of my plate with her knife.

'Come on, dear, eat up.'

As soon as we had finished, she whisked the plates off and I heard her washing them in the kitchen. After a meal she always has to clean up straight away. She came back with two cups of coffee and a Kit-Kat balanced on each saucer. After eating her Kit-Kat, she smoothed the silver foil on the table and asked, 'How do you feel?'

I said everyone had told me the grief would heal with time, and I knew that was right, but it hadn't started happening to me yet. I felt terrible, I said, and I began to cry. I felt her take my hand in hers and start to squeeze it between her wrinkled palms. Tears were pouring and I imagined the kohl around my eyes was starting to streak down my face. I wanted a drink but didn't have the energy to go and get it. I was just wishing to myself that I had when I heard her saying, 'Rudi was a strange young man, wasn't he? Of course, you married him, and you love him, and we were all very happy for you, but he was a strange man.'

I looked at her and wondered what was coming.

'Yes, very happy,' she continued, 'very, very happy. Only you have to face it – he's gone and you can't go on moping for ever. You've got to get back to life and you've got to start looking after yourself.'

'But I'm trying, I'm doing my best.'

Our words went backwards and forwards and then

my mum said, 'You must face facts. After I had my trouble with your father, I only got on the road to recovery once I'd faced the facts.'

I was weeping at her bitterness but she thought it was my grief. She kept squeezing my hand to show me that she cared.

'I need something,' I said – I didn't say what – and I went through to the kitchen and got the bottle of Cinzano from the refrigerator.

27

The coroner's court, out beyond Heathrow, was a modern room. The walls were the same fern-green as the crematorium. The coroner wore a suit and half-moon spectacles.

The pathologist's report on Rudi was read aloud. It described the cause of death as a subarachnoid haemorrhage originating from a rupture of the aneurysm at the junction of the middle cerebral artery and the anterior communicating artery.

The coroner pronounced a verdict of death by natural causes and signed his name.

'I need a drink,' I said, when we got outside into the street.

28

After a few drinks in a pub, Mum and I caught the underground home. With the gin and the swaying of the carriage I nodded off, but every time we got to a station I would wake up, and each time this happened I had an identical vision – my mum, bolt upright, handbag firmly grasped to deter muggers, mouth clamped shut.

At Royal Oak where we got out, there was no ticket collector to take our tickets, and as we walked down Porchester Road towards home Mum complained, 'I'd be surprised if anyone ever pays for a ticket nowadays.'

'I always pay for mine.'

'The system is so slipshod, it encourages crime.'

There was a tramp, I noticed, meandering along on our side towards us. He wore trainers, through which his toes showed, and a tatty old double-breasted suit.

'Can you spare us the price of a cup of tea?' he wheezed when he was in front of us. 'Or enough for a bite?'

I was about to open my handbag, when I heard Mum whispering, 'Come on,' and before I knew what was happening she had pulled me away.

'That's what happens when you drink,' she hissed as we got to the corner, jerking her head back in the direction of the tramp.

That does it, I thought. The green man on the crossing had started to flash, and instead of turning towards home, I led her across the road, up Queensway and into Wineways, the off-licence. Inside there was the usual smell of wet cardboard and sour wine. My mum wrinkled up her nose at it.

I asked the Sikh for a bottle of Dubonnet and twenty Marlboro, opened my purse and saw I only had ten pounds left. This was madness. Oh well, I thought, to hell with all the bills, and handed over the money.

When we got home my mum went straight to the bathroom and ran herself a bath, while I went to the fridge and got some ice out. Then I went to the bathroom door.

'Would you like some Dubonnet?' I called. 'It might be nice in your bath.'

'No, thank you.'

I made a drink for myself and went and sat in the living-room. As the glass slowly chilled, I could feel my fingers getting colder and colder . . .

One more day and Mum would be leaving.

Eight

29

The spring of the letter-box sounded as the flap opened and shut. I got up from the breakfast table that Saturday morning and went out into the hall. There was a single brown envelope lying on the doormat, face down. It had 'Bill' written all over it.

I carried the letter back to the table and slit open the back with a knife.

THIRD DEMAND

Dear Mrs Janowski,

We note that you still have not settled your outstanding account. Unless we receive payment within fourteen days we shall be obliged to consult our legal advisers.

We look forward to hearing from you.

Yours sincerely,
J.W. Lambert

I looked at the letter and then I looked at the bill

which was attached behind with a pin. Then I went over to the sideboard, got out the blue loose-leaf file from beside Rudi's ashes which I also kept there, and came back to the table.

I opened the file and took out the papers inside. There were electricity bills, rates bills, telephone bills, gas bills, other bills and two earlier demands from the undertakers. All told, I owed over three thousand pounds.

When Rudi was alive he had looked after our finances. I was happy with this and I never asked what was going on because I assumed everything was under control. From the outside it looked as if our affairs were being managed with cool efficiency.

In fact it was crisis management, as I had now discovered. Rudi had spent wildly on us, on me. The details were all in the bank statements. The manicure set cost him a hundred pounds at Harrods; the cashmere sweater, which came from South Molton Street, cost over two hundred pounds, and so on.

Instead of paying off our debts, Rudi had let them mount up. He was able to get away with it because whenever he needed some money quickly, he had his sideline to turn to. A few stereos, a consignment of quartz digital waches or a batch of perfumes could always be relied on to get us out of trouble. Only now he was gone and that was gone with him, but the debts were still there and they had to be paid.

In my mind I ran through those to whom I could turn for help. My first choice would have been Zeeta, but with her believing our marriage was perfect, to go to her would have been to reveal this wasn't true and that I didn't want to do. Next were Mum, Vicki and Arthur but I reckoned all they could scrape together would be four or five hundred pounds and that wasn't going to be enough. My third choice was Mr Sammi, but the more I imagined it – the grimy office, a lunchtime, myself at the calculator, himself behind his desk, feet up, smoking a Senior Service, and my asking for three thousand pounds – the more convinced I became that it was inconceivable that he would lend such a sum of money, and would furthermore be offended by such a request.

So what were the other possibilities? Could I save by spending on nothing but essentials? A little, but the problem was too big to be tackled that way alone. Perhaps I could start a chain letter? Ha! Another job? What other job? Waitressing? With my feet? Embezzlement? Hardly. The oldest profession? No.

I was back where I had started. The only option seemed to be to get what I could from my family and make small 'good faith' payments supported by pleading letters. The problem with this, however, as I realized, was that one hard-hearted 'No' from one of those to whom I owed money and the whole strategy would tumble down like a house of cards. This was the moment, having gone through all the options, that I thought about someone I'd been hoarding for a emergency like this – my last chance.

His name was Claus. I met him just after I had come back to live in London, and our affair had lasted a year. And since it ended I hadn't seen him, unless you counted spotting his photograph once in *Harper's*

Claus is German. His parents came over to Manchester in the middle 1930s. They were not Jews but socialists. He was born in 1936.

When the war ended his parents remained until he had finished school. They then returned to Germany, but their son, having put down roots in this country, decided to remain. His father being an art dealer, Claus followed him into the business, eventually coming to London and opening a gallery

I met him like this. I was taken to a party in a big house in St John's Wood. There was a marquee in the garden and a band of Mexican trumpeters. There were two little girls there, blonde-haired and self-confident. I started talking to them and that in turn led to meeting their father. Claus was in his late forties and recently separated. At weekends he had the girls.

He had a lovely smile and lovely teeth. He always woke up before I did and would get out of bed, leaving me to wake alone and slowly, which is what I like. When we went away for the weekend, he'd take me on long walks and tell me stories about his favourite painters. All that time I was with him I loved him, although what exactly his feelings were towards me it was hard to know exactly.

We went abroad, twice. The first time was to the South of France. Each evening we sat on our balcony and drank cassis, overlooking a golden sea with the sun setting over it. Our other trip was to the Swiss Alps. On the second day I twisted the cartilage in my knee while skiing and afterwards spent my days alone and miserable in the chalet. In the evenings Claus's friends came over and they all spoke German with one another.

The argument didn't start until Zürich airport, and then continued throughout the flight. I complained I

154

had been ignored and not spoken to for a week. He replied that I was a type, like ivy. I could only grow if I was supported by someone else and I was destructive. My roots would eventually get into the masonry and cause the building which was supporting me to fall down. All the way into London in the taxi we did not speak a word, and when I got out all we could manage was a curt goodbye to each other.

A week or so later, we met for tea in the Fountain bar underneath Fortnum & Mason. I had a present for him – a pair of gold cuff-links inscribed with his initials – C.S.

He told me it was over. I had not expected this. There had been a reconciliation, he explained, and he was going to be with his wife for Christmas. I asked if I could telephone him in the country and wish him happy Christmas. He refused. I asked to be left alone. He went, leaving his cuff-links. I wept, my big tears falling on the tablecloth. An old waitress with crooked teeth asked if I was all right and held my wrist in her hand.

It wouldn't last with the wife, I believed. If I could just hold on, he'd come back to me. But a few days later I got a card. There was a picture on the front of the Three Wise Men and it was signed Claus and Emily. I tore it up instantly.

Christmas followed – endless walks along dripping lanes with Arthur, Vicki and the twins, cheap crackers with the same joke in every one (we wrote and complained but never got a reply), the Queen's message and indigestion.

Sometime in the New Year his wife Emily went away

somewhere and Claus got lonely. He rang and asked me to supper and like a fool I agreed. We went to Wheeler's in Kensington and of course we drank more than we ought and we ended up going over the road to the Royal Garden Hotel. As soon as I took my clothes off, my period started. His semen tasted woody and got into my hair.

The next morning he said, 'If ever you're in trouble, you can always come to me.'

It was the end of the end and I knew it.

I fetched a pen and a pad and wrote the letter straight off.

Dear Claus

I am sorry to be writing to you like this after such a long gap.

You may know that I got married; well, I am now a widow. My husband died a couple of months ago. He was thirty-three.

It is a long time since we saw each other, but I still haven't forgotten what you said the last time. I could always come to you if I was in trouble, you said.

Well, I am in trouble. Can I come to you?

You can reach me at this address above, or ring me at work if you prefer (289 3573)

I'd love to hear from you,

       With love,
       Catherine

30

There was a blue sky overhead with a thin veil of cloud lying underneath it, like a stretched piece of gauze. I dropped my letter to Claus into the Westbourne Grove letter-box and heard it land in the wire basket inside. The road beside me was choked with cars, their roofs, bumpers and windscreens all shining in the pale sunshine.

Then I headed towards the chemist's. Tidying up my purse the Friday evening before, I had come across a ticket stub for a roll of film which I had dropped in a few days before Rudi's death, and forgotten about since then.

I pushed open the chemist's door feeling slightly apprehensive. The idea of collecting these photographs had been with me since I woke up, and hovered on the edge of my thoughts all the time since, even as I'd been writing the letter. It had been with me as I had dressed afterwards to come out, and as I had dropped the letter into the box. I had a vague idea this was a roll which contained pictures of our wedding and which had got mislaid afterwards. If these were the pictures then I wanted them, but I was also frightened of what they would stir up if they were them.

Walking across the floor of the chemist's I stiffened my resolve by reminding myself, this was just another piece of unfinished business which had to be tidied up. And hadn't there been others? Rudi's laundry, for instance (which I had done carefully – I could hardly give his tee-shirts to Oxfam when they were dirty), collecting the alarm clock he'd left at the menders, and sorting out his National Insurance.

'Yes?' said the girl behind the counter, tall, with hennaed hair, and a purse on a string which cut between her breasts. I recognized her from when I'd dropped the roll in.

I gave her the docket and after rummaging in a box she produced one of those glossy packets which the laboratories return photographs in, with a picture on the front of a blond father carrying his blonde daughter on his shoulders, his perfect blonde wife walking beside him, holding the hand of their perfect blond son.

I paid and took the packet over to a stretch of empty counter near a carousel where there were sunglasses on display. I had to see what was inside immediately. Who can resist looking at their pictures the moment they get them back? I opened the seal and reached in for the photographs. They came out upside down. I turned them over, my heart beating.

The very first photograph was of our wedding breakfast in the King of Siam – it was the roll we had mislaid – all the guests around the table, their glasses raised.

I quickly shuffled on. Besides wedding pictures (bride, groom, best man), there were domestic pictures (myself lying in the bath reading *Marie Claire*, cutting my fringe, Rudi washing up), nude pictures (it was an afternoon we had gone to bed, and after undressing, as I was pulling the curtains, I heard 'Smile, beautiful' and turned to find Rudi with the camera), family pictures (Vicki, Arthur, the twins, mum, Tiffany), fancy dress pictures (Rudi and I dressed as 'The Gangster and his Moll' at Zeeta's fancy dress fiftieth birthday), domestic pictures (the flat, the view from the window of the Westway), and pictures of Rudi (asleep and standing on the steps of St Paul's, staring into the lens with his watery blue eyes).

This picture of Rudi was the last in the pile, and the moment I saw it I remembered the moment I had clicked the shutter that day, and had known as I had done so that I had got his look exactly. Now as I stared down at it I felt a stab inside – and this was a surprise to me, for I had expected the pictures of the wedding to upset me, not this – but seeing him so alive and as he was, brought it home to me with especial acuteness that he was dead. From there I slid into self-pity, for what I thought about then was that he would never saunter into the flat of an evening ever again, a *London Standard* under his arm, a film he wanted us to see ringed in biro, and worse, I wasn't ever going to hold him again. I felt another stab of pain, a stronger one. So what did you expect? I reproached myself. To collect these and remain untouched? You wanted them, didn't you? You want every scrap from your lives together, don't you?

I started to cry.

The assistant came over, the string with the purse cutting between her breasts, and asked, 'Are you all right?'

I rallied and wiped my nose on the cuff of my jacket and said, 'Thank you, I'll be all right in a moment.'

She slid away, and pretending to be tidying the bottles of shampoo on a shelf a few feet off, she kept looking at me. I found a tissue in my pocket and blew my nose. Then I turned to the carousel, which I knew would have a mirror, so that I could see how I looked. There was a man there, trying on some sunglasses – I had been vaguely aware of him all the time I had been looking at the photographs – and at the moment I turned he removed the pair of sunglasses he had been trying on and I saw he was smiling at me.

'Hello,' he said.

As I wiped my eyes again the assistant came back and asked, 'Do you know one another?' There was an audible tone of relief in her voice.

'Yes we do,' said the man, and suddenly I recognized him as the one from the off-licence who had followed me into the café the night Rudi died, and talked to me.

I heard him saying quietly, 'Let's go outside.' I felt his hand on my elbow and let him steer me towards the door. When we were outside he said, 'I'm Johnnie Pashley. Do you remember me?'

I nodded.

'We could go back to that café. Would you like that? It's near here, isn't it? Just up Queensway.'

I nodded again.

'It was all right, wasn't it?'

'Oh yes, absolutely.'

31

In the Blue Sky café the seats have rounded edges, the tables are formica and blue, and the walls, floor and ceiling are blue as well. Inside is a little like being in a swimming pool, circa 1950.

We went to the back room where it is quieter than at the front. There is no counter here, just a hatch through which the plates get shuffled in and out.

We ordered cappuccinos. George brought them through and put them in front of us with a grunt. Johnnie put a neat mound of sugar on his spoon and tipped it slowly, so that instead of making a hole in the froth, the grains passed straight through. I just threw my sugar in and stirred the top away.

It was a warm day and George had opened the side door on to the lane. In the air there were little hovering specks of grime lit up by the sunshine.

'Have you read any good books lately?' I asked politely, remembering what it said on the card in my purse – he was a bookseller.

He looked across at me and blinked, turning the gold signet ring on his little finger, then smiled suddenly, showing his white teeth with their neat gap between the middle two.

'I never read the damn things. I just sell them. I deal in rare books. I buy and sell from collectors and specialists. I'm selling an enormous natural history collection at the moment.'

We talked about what each of us did and then he said, 'What's in here?' He picked up the photographs saying, 'Can I?' and I nodded to him. Then he took the pictures out and started to shuffle through them, asking questions from time to time about who people were.

'Very interesting,' he said when he had finished, looking as if he was about to return them to the envelope, but then it was as if he changed his mind for he began to go through them again, studying each one closely and carefully except for the one where I was pulling the curtain closed. This he shuffled on without looking at it.

'How are you feeling?' he asked when he had finished, tidying the pictures into a neat block like a deck of cards and sliding them back into the envelope. I told him and he asked another question which I answered, which led on to another question and another answer, and slowly I found myself telling him everything that had happened since Rudi died and how I felt, the worst part of which were the moods. These were like a fog which wrapped around me. I could not see out through them and when I was in one, I was dark, silent and morose. I would have to drag myself out of bed. I would have to drag myself to work. I would have to drag myself through the day. When I came home in the evening I would feel drained. It would be an effort to eat. I didn't even feel like having a drink. I would go to bed early, exhausted, but then as soon as my head hit the pillow my mind would start to whirl and I wouldn't be able to sleep.

These would last a day, two days. Then, they would go. I could go off to work in the depths of one and by afternoon it would have lifted. I'd come home in the evening and I'd be more my old self. I'd bring flowers. I'd cook myself dinner. There was still the pain, of course, but I didn't feel locked in with it.

And over the months, I told him, I'd come to see these moods as an illness. Unfortunately, I couldn't take anything to make them go away. Only time could work that miracle, and in the end, it always did.

Johnnie nodded understandingly as he listened. When I finished he was quiet. He didn't ask questions and he didn't try to cheer me up either, just stared without blinking from behind his steel-rimmed spectacles and nodded, and I knew then he had understood.

Several coffees later Johnnie asked, 'Would you like to come out one evening?' and suggested a date and a time.

'I don't know if I know you well enough to say yes,' I said.

'I gave you my card, but why don't I give you my address again?' he said.

He wrote it out in a small black notebook. He used a fountain pen and then blew on the page to dry the ink. Then he tore the page out and gave it to me.

Outside on the pavement he said, 'I'd like to see you whenever you're ready. You have my number now. The ball's in your court. Do telephone. You've got the number. We could have some fun.'

I was in the dark. It was so dark I couldn't see. There

was a high wall and I was running along beside it. I had my hand on the bricks. I had to get to the other side. As I couldn't get over, I would have to get through. I was feeling for a door or a window.

I ran on and on. The skin on my hand got sore. There weren't any doors or windows.

Gradually I realized the wall ran in a circle and I was running in a circle as I followed it round. I would never be able to get to the other side.

I gave up my searching and began walking along slowly. I started to cry. At that moment I heard a voice.

'Clarissa, Clarissa,' it called, which was my name in the dream. Why Clarissa when I am Catherine? I don't know.

I looked up and saw Johnnie standing on the wall above me, holding a candle. There was a wind blowing and he had one hand cupped around the flame to stop it going out.

'Come on,' he said, 'come up.'

I wanted to get up but I couldn't get up there unless he helped me. The trouble was, in order to give me a hand he would have to put the candle down, and he couldn't do that because then it would blow out.

That was the end. I was on the ground, he was on the wall, and I was looking up at him.

I had this dream soon after Johnnie found me crying in the chemist's.

Nine

32

In the middle of the 7-Eleven on Praed Street, where I had gone to get milk and biscuits for our morning coffee, a young black man in a filthy coat and broken spectacles stood staring at the floor, refusing to answer the manager's questions. He wasn't a drunk but a patient from a hospital. He was obviously harmless and yet everybody, including myself, felt nervous of him as we moved about the shop.

Just as I was leaving, a police car pulled up outside and two policemen got out, and through the shop windows I caught sight of them as I walked away, marching the young black man towards the door. All the 7-Eleven employees in their striped shirts and black hats were watching intently, and when the police got the man out through the door they applauded.

As I came into the Praed Street Cleaners, Mabel reared up from behind the counter.

'Roll on six o'clock,' she said, scowled and ducked down again.

She'd dropped her box of pins and there were

thousands of them on the floor which Eric was helping her to pick up.

'Cup of tea?' asked Mabel coaxingly as I looked down on them. 'We're not having a very good morning in here. Oh, and by the way, there was a phone call for you,' she added.

'You know what would be favourite for these pins?' observed Eric. 'A magnet.'

'Stop your gabbing and get on with it,' urged Mabel humorously. Standing and then turning, she handed one of our dockets to me, and on the back in her square, heavy handwriting was written:

Claus – 352 8741

I dialled the number and it rang three or four times before it was picked up. I heard a bored female saying, 'Yes?'

'Is that the Nine Lives gallery?'

'Yes.'

'Can I speak to Claus, please?'

'I don't think he's in. Hang on . . . . Anyone know where Claus is lurking?' I heard the girl shouting at the other end. After a pause she returned. 'I'm afraid there doesn't seem to be any sign . . .' she began and then a male voice cut in and said, 'Of course I'm here. I was on the other line.'

'This is Catherine,' I said.

'Oh, hello. How are you?' I heard him saying, and then he continued, 'What a long time it's been.'

'That's true.'

'I got your letter this morning,' he said and then he continued, speaking to someone in the room, 'I'm on the phone. Will you *please* close the door.

'I was saying, I got your letter,' he repeated, speaking softly and sounding sympathetic. 'It must have been a terrible blow to you.'

'It did come as a shock.'

'Look, I don't think the phone is the best place to discuss this. Do you?'

'No.'

'I'm awfully busy at the moment. Well, I'm always awfully busy. I can't do it today. Look, could you do tomorrow? It's Saturday and I'm in the gallery as it so happens. Could you come after lunch? Say, half-past three?'

Ten

33

Through my bedroom window I saw a sky with patches of blue and big white fluffy clouds. I opened my wardrobe and chose a dress. The material was silky and printed with a pattern of little flowers. I added a black jacket and my favourite flat black shoes and a pair of pearl earrings I had bought in Bahrain. Then I looked at myself. I was stylish but not overdressed. When I have to do something difficult I must look right. I can't do it if I'm not.

I came out of my bedroom and into the hall. I had just dabbed on some perfume and its thick scent hung around me.

On the stairway I could smell the drains, mixed with the odour of frying fat which lingers in Westbourne Mansions all the year round.

In the courtyard, the yapping of Mrs Small's dog faithfully followed me, but the moment I stepped into Bishop's Bridge Road, Tommy's yelps were drowned by the roar of the traffic. Though it was summer, there was a cold breeze, lifting grit from the pavement and blowing it along in clouds.

I walked to the corner and crossed over to Queensway. The wind was stronger here, and I had to screw up my eyes as I walked towards the underground.

Outside Bayswater station there was a tramp standing silently amongst the crowds. He was wearing a drab, dirty suit which only a tramp would wear, and his trouser bottoms and cuffs were seriously frayed. He was holding out a trilby and flicking it from side to side, the way cats swish their tails. This was meant to attract money from passers-by but in fact the action was so obscure, no one was paying any attention.

Drawing closer, I saw there were only two pennies in the bottom and so I opened my handbag to find my purse. Sometimes when you stop near a beggar they have a quick look at you (not too long a look, of course, in case it puts you off), and you can see the hope in their eyes, but not this one. All the hope had been ground out of him.

I put all the coppers and all the silver I had in his old green trilby and went on.

I caught the Circle Line train to Sloane Square and came out on to the King's Road. Being Saturday, the pavements were jammed. It wasn't quite half-past two. I was an hour early. There was time to settle myself.

I started walking down Sloane Street away from the crowds. I like the mansion blocks built of pink brick but the new barracks further down were horrible. There were pale soldiers outside, no more than boys, in ridiculous bearskin hats. A sergeant was shouting at them.

At the bottom I turned on to Chelsea Embankment. There was a parapet wall made of stone. It was black with the filth of London. After walking a little way I stopped and leant on it. The river was in and sloshed against the wall some feet below. The dark water reminded me of the black powder-paint I mixed as a child at school. On the edges of the Thames lay a yellow froth.

Then, for no reason at all, I remembered the man with the green trilby hat standing outside Bayswater station. For as long as I can remember there have been beggars on the streets of London. In the past they were either in railway stations, or they hung around the West End where they could beg from tourists, or they were in the East End on the old bomb sites, but now they're everywhere. They're in the underground, shivering and scratching in the carriages; they're on every street corner with bottles of cider, yelling out for money to anyone who looks at them; and they're in the parks and on the commons, sitting around fires which light up their terrible faces.

The money made at the top, I hear, is trickling down to the ones at the bottom. Everyone is better off, I hear, the poor as well as the rich. It doesn't look like that where I stand. The poor are getting poorer, I thought, watching the river as it flowed at my feet. That reminded me of the money I had to find. Three thousand? Probably closer to four thousand now. It was outrageous.

Then I thought, I am closer to the man with the trilby hat than I know, my lips speaking the thought as if I were actually speaking it. I felt faint and giddy. Think about something else, I thought. I started walking on. The wind was still blowing and I was cold. I wished I'd brought something warm, my cashmere, the mauve one Rudi gave me. Where the wind caught it, the Thames was ruffled like gathered cloth.

To get my mind off things I listened to my footsteps, I stared at passing pedestrians, and at one point I stopped to look at one of the old lamp standards. At the bottom the stem turned into enormous lion's paws. Who ever heard of a lamp coming out of an animal's foot. It made me laugh.

Somewhere near the Royal Hospital, there was an ice-cream van parked by the kerb. It was decorated with pictures of space rockets and planets and stars. On the back was written 'There goes Toni' and no doubt on the front was written 'Here comes Toni'. No one was buying. It was too cold.

The driver was standing in the serving window with his arms folded. He was looking out, not seeing anything.

'It can't be all that bad,' I called out to him.

'Don't you believe it, darling,' he said, 'it's worse.'

34

The plate on the door read 'Nine Lives'. There was a cat beside the words, sitting on its haunches, and it looked like it had got the cream.

I pushed the door open, went in and found myself in a huge white gallery with pictures hanging on the walls. There was a wooden floor and overhead a series of big skylights.

The office area was at the rear. A young woman was sitting behind a typewriter at a designer glass table. A man was lazing nearby on a deck-chair. There were some scupltures on the floor and these two were looking at them.

'I'm afraid we're closed,' the young woman said, getting up and coming towards me.

I recognized the voice straight away. She was the one who had answered the telephone.

'Lo, I'm going to help myself to a fag, okay?' the man called after her. He was in his early twenties, with a long black pony-tail and a mournful face.

'I'm afraid we're closed,' the young woman repeated.

Lo, as she was called, had a slim body and large breasts which she stuck out proudly. She was wearing a loose short skirt with a print of red roses on it, just a bit too close for comfort to the pattern on my dress. On the top of her long hair rested a pair of sunglasses.

'I have an appointment.'

'I'm sorry. Who are you?'

'My name is Catherine Janowski.'

'I'm expecting her,' called Claus, leaning out of a door at the far end of the room while holding a telephone. 'I'll be as quick as I can,' he added apologetically.

Claus shut his door and I went and sat on a church pew against the back wall. The sculptures were on a sheet on the floor, and they were the work, I presumed, of the young man called Freddie on the deck-chair. They all comprised of shapes like eggs, with sections of their shells cut away to reveal that inside there were other eggs with other eggs inside them, or sometimes other objects – a diving mask, a claw hammer, a packet of screws. The pieces were all painted, greens, greys and blues mostly.

'Listen to this,' said Freddie, reading from a newspaper which was open to his lap. 'A search is on in Naples for a rogue taxi driver who preys on single women. He takes them to the countryside, strips them of their clothes and possessions and then leaves them to make their way home.'

Lo laughed.

'Do you believe that?' Freddie took a slow deep puff and exhaled.

'No. I think it's the same as those stories about old ladies with hairy hands who are meant to lurk with big cleavers in underground car parks.'

'You mean,' said Freddie, putting on a funny voice, 'this is an urban myth which expresses our deepest fears.'

178

'Come on, let's go,' said Lo, putting a piece of paper in the typewriter.

I listened as Freddie slowly dictated his biography and Lo typed it out. Born Limerick, 1958 . . . art college in Dublin . . . four years in Barcelona . . . shows in Belfast, Leeds, Limoges, Kinsale, Birmingham . . .

I looked down to the window at the far end. There was an elm tree outside and I could see its green and brown bark. It looked as though it was made of pieces of torn paper laid on top of each other.

One of Freddie's egg things, I thought, would probably take care of my entire financial predicament.

35

The door opened and Claus stuck his head out and said, 'Come in.'

His office was small and drab, with dusty security bars over the windows and an old safe in the wall with the royal coat of arms on the half-open door. Outside the window was a small garden full of weeds and piles of earth.

'How are you?' he asked.

Claus was changed since I had known him. He was older, he was over fifty now, and plumper, which didn't suit him because he is short, and there were streaks of grey in his beard. He kissed my cheek and that too was different from what I remembered.

After the kiss he put his arms around my shoulders, I put my arms around his back, and we pressed each other lightly. I kept my eyes wide open and stared over his shoulder towards the safe.

We separated. Claus went to his place and I sat on a leather armchair in front of the desk. Then Claus looked across at me.

'When did we last see each other?' he asked. 'It was here, wasn't it?'

He lit a new cigarette from the one he had going and put the old one out. The ashtray was a big square slab filled with sand from out of which his old stubs stuck up like shoots.

'No,' I said, 'the last time we met wasn't here.'

He'd been in a different gallery then. He'd forgotten that.

'Surely the last time was here? What was it we were showing? Christ, let me think.'

He struck his forehead with the flat of his palm.

'No,' I said quietly, 'I was never here.'

The last time we had seen each other was one morning outside the Royal Garden Hotel in Kensington, where we had gone to spend the night after too much to drink at dinner the evening before. After saying goodbye, he headed off towards the park. He lived on the other side at the time and he was going to walk home. I pointed myself the other way, towards the underground.

It was early and there was a dense mist. You couldn't hear the sound of the traffic properly through it.

'Cheer up,' an Irish boy called to me, as I was crawling down the ramp from the hotel to the street and he was walking up it.

I got as far as Kensington High Street underground station and then I turned round and ran back after Claus. I hadn't a clue what I would say when I caught up with him. I hadn't a clue what I would do. All I could think was, I've got to find him. I've got to see him. I've got to hold him.

I ran through the dripping gate into Kensington Gardens. The board with the by-laws was there like a gibbet, also dripping. The path in front of me was dripping. It disappeared into the white mist like a road in a fairytale.

I started forward. I was straining my eyes and ears. Every time someone loomed out of the fog my heart would race. But it was never him.

Eventually I found a bench, sat down and started to cry. A man in a track suit came up and asked me if I was all right. I nodded, got up and hurried away from him.

I went on a few feet and then it struck me. Perhaps this man had seen Claus? I turned around but of course the mist had swallowed him up.

I was wet through and miserable and it was futile to continue. I turned and began to make my way back towards the gate.

'Tell me what's been happening,' Claus said gently.

I described first the Registry Office marriage and when Rudi and I started to live together. Then I described the awful days and weeks and months since his death, and as I told Claus about each thing, I felt again what I'd felt when I'd lived it, and before long I had quite forgotten what I had come to ask for.

Then suddenly he wasn't giving me his full attention any more but glancing down at the light winking on the top of the telephone.

'Hang on,' he said, and rising from his chair and hurrying towards the door he shouted, 'Lo, line two.' As he reached for the handle the door opened and Lo was outside.

'It's Jim Armstrong,' she said.

'What a damned time to ring,' he said and picked up the telephone.

'Yes.'

'. . .'

'Where the hell are you?'

'. . .'

'Guinea what? I sent you to bloody Mali.'

In my head I rehearsed the words . . . I need a thousand pounds. I desperately need a thousand pounds.

Lo offered me a glass and I took it. There was warm white wine in it. I began to drink. I was vaguely aware that Claus was having a long and unpleasant argument. His artist was in the wrong country at the wrong time. A revolution had started and he had lost all his – or, to be accurate, Claus's – money.

I finished the glass quickly and took another and then a third from the bottle on the desk in front of me. Now there was alcohol flowing in my veins, new words began to sound in my head . . . Dear, sweet Claus, don't you understand why I've come to see you? We had nothing put aside. Rudi and I were your classic spendthrifts. Owned nothing. Saved nothing. Please, Claus, not a thousand, no, four thousand will clear it. No. five thousand and then I can start with a clean slate.

More wine. The bars over the windows were sagging and the room was swaying. Claus came off the phone.

'Every day is worse than the day before,' I said, 'and you think it can't get worse than this and then the next day it is.'

I need your money, I thought. 'I'm broke,' I said.

I noticed the wine in my glass was red. So was the bottle on the desk.

'Wasn't it white before?' I said.

The bottles had been changed and I hadn't noticed.

183

'Do you need money?' he asked.

No, I'll work harder. I'll borrow from Mr Sammi. I'll get some from Zeeta. I'll borrow from my friends.

But Mr Sammi was never going to give me any. And I was damned if I was going begging to Zeeta with the sorry tale of my idiocy and Rudi's stupidity. My own family hadn't anything. He really was my only chance. I'd never get the money anywhere else.

'I've got to pay for the funeral,' I said, slurring ever so slightly, 'and I haven't got it.'

The other bills I decided not mention until later.

Claus was standing beside me. He put his arms around me and I put my head against him. Then the man in Guinea-Bissau rang again.

A few minutes later, I found myself in the street with Lo and Freddie.

'He'll see you at ten tonight,' said Lo, speaking slightly more slowly than usual on account of my state. 'Here are the details,' she said, and she put a card, with what I presumed was the address, into my handbag. 'And here's your fare,' she continued and she pressed a crinkly fifty-pound note into my palm and helped me into the waiting taxi.

The inside of the black cab smelt of disinfectant. We drove off. The street passed outside the window in a blur.

I got home and up to my flat. It was silent and safe. I climbed into bed without undressing and fell into a deep sleep.

Eleven

36

I woke up. I looked at my wristwatch. It was seven o'clock. My dress was crumpled.

I ran a bath. I lay in the hot water, watching the drips falling from the end of the hot tap. My head started to clear. Thoughts came. I decided what I would wear. I chose a green dress with short sleeves and a high collar.

I was able to hail a taxi immediately on Bishop's Bridge Road. I took this as a good omen for the evening ahead. Everything was going to work out fine.

I looked at the card Lo had put into my handbag and called out the address to the driver. After he divorced, Claus had moved from Bayswater up to Primrose Hill. I remembered reading about it somewhere.

We passed under the Westway and drove alongside the canal towards St John's Wood. I looked out of the window at the huge houses of the wealthy and thought how lovely it would be to live in one.

I was floating ten feet above the ground. It felt great to be alive and to be going somewhere on Saturday night.

*   *   *

At Primrose Hill the cab turned up at the side of the park. Beyond the railings I could see the lamps along the paths glowing in the darkness. We had arrived, 35 Marlbank seemed very familiar to me somehow. It was a big white stucco house with an old-fashioned rocking-horse in the window.

Had I been in this street before? Perhaps to a party? I couldn't remember.

I walked across the pavement to a wooden door which was set in a wall and was open. I went through and found myself in a paved front garden filled with green flower-tubs. In front of me there was a high house with wide windows. It was white and it gleamed like icing. No, I hadn't been here before.

Like the gate, the front door was open. I went in without ringing the bell. In the hall there was a hat-stand with a clutch of umbrellas, a table and an ink-well.

In front of me there was a door and a set of stairs leading to the next floor. The door was open and I heard Claus shouting from beyond it, 'Come in, come in.'

I followed the sound of his voice until I found myself in an enormous living-room with three big french windows at the back and the rocking-horse at the front.

'So you found your way in,' he said.

Claus was kneeling on the floor. He had a large black speaker for a record-player in front of him and he was attaching a wire to the back of it.

'I'm updating my hi-fi,' he explained. Before I could reply he continued, 'You know, I was so angry this afternoon with Jim – you remember, the one on the telephone?'

188

I nodded.

'Another of my good deeds, sending him off to paint, and he goes to the wrong fucking country. Then there's some sort of a coup and all his money goes. And I'm the one who has to bail him out. This afternoon was very expensive, I can tell you.

'Anyway, on the way home tonight, I thought, Claus, you've had a hard day. So I went up Tottenham Court Road, went into Lasky's or somewhere and said, "I want the best stereo money can buy." And here it is.'

I looked down at the deck and the amplifier, the boxes and the polystyrene packing lying about on the floor.

'You look marvellous,' he said, and stood up and kissed me on the cheeks. 'I wish I'd dressed up a bit,' he continued, 'and wasn't so scruffy.' He was in a boiler suit: white, starched and immaculately ironed.

I smiled.

He fetched a large jug of Pimm's, filled with clinking ice and mint, from the kitchen.

'Make yourself at home,' he said, handing me a full glass.

I took it and went to the huge sofa piled with Turkish cushions. The little bubbles in the lemonade pricked my mouth when I took my first mouthful. I felt thirsty and drank the rest greedily.

'Would you like another?' he asked when I had finished, and I held my tumbler out.

'Are you feeling better tonight?' he called, as he tipped the jug towards my glass. I noticed his glass was still on the small table where he'd left it and it was almost untouched.

'Oh, yes, thank you. I had a bit too much wine.'

'Perhaps you needed it.'

He handed my glass back to me.

'You must have thought I was an idiot this afternoon,' he continued.

I shrugged.

'All that stuff, "When did we last meet? Surely it was in the gallery, et cetera, et cetera." After you left I remembered of course. I felt very embarrassed.'

He looked at me and I wondered at that moment whether what he remembered was simply our saying goodbye or whether he remembered, for instance, walking through Kensington Gardens in the mist.

I am sure that at that time he had felt relieved the affair was over but I also want to believe he was sad about it. But had he imagined, as he went home, that I would follow him and try to make a scene? Now, as I thought about it, I imagined that yes, he probably did, and I imagined he walked very fast through the mist, little beads of sweat forming on his brow as he hurried along. No wonder he had forgotten about it.

I thought all this in no time at all and the next moment was when I decided I would let myself get drunk.

'I need a thousand pounds,' I said, 'for the undertaker. But really, I need four thousand, for all the other bills.'

With the drink I was quite unselfconscious now.

'Hang on. How much do you need exactly?' He lit a cigarette and opened the pad on his knee. 'You said the undertaker's was seven hundred and twenty-one pounds.'

Did I?

I remembered telling him my life story, but had I given him figures as well?

'It is,' I admitted, 'but then there's VAT and the flowers and everything else on top.'

My mind went blank, I drained my glass and looked into the bottom.

'Why don't you help yourself,' he said.

I took off my shoes and walked across the floor. I took long strides and rose up on my toes with each step.

At the drinks table I turned my back on him so he couldn't see what I was doing. I filled my glass three-quarters full with brandy and then added a splash of soda.

'What do you need all the rest of the money for?' he asked.

I took a mouthful from my glass. It was almost undiluted. Instead of bubbles pricking my mouth, there was the strong taste of spirit.

'You haven't told me. What do you need three thousand-odd pounds for?' he repeated.

I swallowed the brandy and shivered.

I said, 'Everything's going to be cut off, phone, gas, electricity, any day now.'

I refilled the glass with Pimm's.

As I returned to my place, the polished wooden floor felt slippery underfoot.

'Let's talk about something else,' I said brightly.

I told him that from as far back as I could remember, I'd always found that that time of year, the early summer, made me feel sad as well as happy.

When I looked at the first buds or the first leaves I

191

said, as I did every spring. I couldn't stop myself thinking, They're going to die in a few months. They're going to be dead before Christmas because it's their destiny. From the moment they start to grow it's their fate. From even before they start to grow.

Throughout my monologue I kept refilling my glass. My mood was changing. When I'd arrived I'd been up. Now I was sinking.

'I musn't dwell too much on this sort of stuff,' I said loudly. 'If I do, I start getting maudlin and I hate that.'

'Let's put on a record,' he suggested, 'and try this system out. You choose.'

I chose Ella Fitzgerald singing, 'I Love Paris in the Springtime'.

Big mistake.

The moment her voice started I began to cry. The room whirled round and round. My eyelids drooped. My head sank on to the sofa.

'Come on,' I heard Claus saying.

I was on my feet. My arm was over his shoulder and he was supporting me. He walked me across the living-room and took me through a door. I saw a vast bed with a black bedspread. I saw a painting of a vase with flowers in it. I saw an old lampshade with beads hanging from it.

'This is the guest-room. I'm going to put you in here.'

We were at the edge of the bed and he pulled back the covers. I saw the clean, stretched undersheet. It was a field of snow. I would tumble head-first down into it and it would be cool. I would gently go numb. I would fall asleep and I might never wake up again.

'I'm just going to take your dress off,' he said.

I heard him undoing the zip and then I felt the dress dropping to the floor.

What a fool you are.

The words drummed over and over and over in my head. That's the awful part of drink. One moment you're in a lovely field of snow, and the next moment you're hating yourself.

I tipped forward and my head was suddenly on the pillow . . .

My mother was lifting my legs on to the bed and pulling the covers over me . . .

No, it wasn't my mother . . . It was Claus.

'Good night,' he said.

By the time he turned off the light I was asleep.

37

I opened my eyes. I was on my side. I was curled up in a ball like a baby. This wasn't the room with the black bedspread, or the painting of the flowers in the vase, or the old lampshade. This was a room with bookshelves filled with thick books, an old table, and a metal sculpture. This was not where I had fallen asleep. This was another room.

As I tried to account for this, my gaze wandered to the french windows and then to the washing-line outside. There was a duvet cover hanging over it, and a sheet, and a huge black oblong which looked suspiciously like the cover from the bed the night before. The french windows were slightly ajar. Mingled with the cold air wafting in from the garden was the unmistakable sour-vinegar smell of sick.

Oh dear God, I thought, I didn't, did I? I couldn't have? Oh yes I had, I remembered, I had thrown up in the guest room.

Something moved. There was someone else beside me in the bed, and what was more, I realized, I was naked. Oh yes – it was all coming back to me – in the middle of the night I had vomited, like there had been no tomorrow, all over the bed and myself. Claus had undressed me and showered me, and then I had got into the only dry bed left, which was his, where I had immediately fallen into a deep sleep.

I turned and saw Claus. He was leaning against his pillows, reading a book. On his bare chest there were grey hairs among the black ones.

He said, 'Good morning. How are you feeling?'

I began, 'I feel absolutely . . .' but couldn't finish off.

I put on a thick towelling dressing-gown and followed Claus out to the kitchen. I took the glass of freshly squeezed orange juice which he gave me and said, 'Thank you.'

Bacon hissed under the grill. Claus cracked eggs into a pan. I heard a key turning in the front door of the flat. A cleaner? This hour on a Sunday? Footsteps were coming down the hall towards us.

'Oh hello,' said Claus from the stove. He was beating the eggs.

'Good morning, sport,' I heard.

Then the man who had come into the kitchen started staring at me and I thought, I know this man. I know this square body and the square head which sits on top of it. I know those green eyes. I know that forehead where the flesh is heavy and lined. I know that gold signet ring on the little finger. It was Johnnie Pashley.

'Oh, hello.' He looked astonished and then he said, sounding a little piqued, 'How do you two know each other?'

How do you explain a situation like this? How do you say, I know what you're thinking but it's not true?

Claus turned to me. 'This is an old girlfriend,

Catherine. And this Catherine, is the man who lives upstairs, Johnnie.'

Johnnie took a packet of grissini sticks out of the cupboard and said, 'We've met.'

Claus gave the eggs a stir. 'Oh yes. How's that?' It was a bland-sounding inquiry.

'We met in an off-licence, didn't we?'

'Wineways.'

'That's right, in Queensway. Well done that girl for remembering the name.'

He broke a stick in two and bit one end.

I said, 'You saved me from a very unpleasant Alsatian.'

'Did I? I don't remember that.' He did a little swagger with his heavy head and shoulders. 'I never remember my good deeds.'

'What a small world it is,' said Claus, peppering the eggs.

Johnnie offered a bread stick to me like a cigarette and I took it.

'However, we've done all our socializing,' said Johnnie, 'not in the off-licence, but a few doors away in the Blue Sky café. Also off Queensway. Best cappuccinos in West London.'

'Sorry, mate, got to correct you there,' said Claus, shaking his head, 'Bar Italia, Frith Street.'

'Anything you say, boss.'

Then Claus turned to me. 'Tell me, Catherine, because I'm not going to get a straight answer from him,' and he jerked his thumb in Johnnie's direction, 'what's he doing down in Queensway? Godforsaken spot. Full of tarts and Arabs. Nothing to recommend it.'

'A Greek Orthodox priest in Moscow Road has a very

large natural history collection,' said Johnnie, 'and I'm helping him to realize its value.'

Claus handed me three plates and the knives and forks. 'Oh, I bet you are.' We all laughed together.

The food was on the plate in front of me. I took a mouthful straight away. The omelette was piping hot. I couldn't swallow it. I couldn't spit it out either. So it stayed there, on my tongue, while I panted like a dog. Claus and Johnnie both looked up and then went back to buttering their toast.

I swallowed and started to ask my questions. I gathered they had become friends after 'my time', and bought the house together when Claus finally left his wife for good.

Everywhere coincidences, if you only know where to look for them.

38

I followed Claus into his bedroom after breakfast. He opened the drawer of a chest. There was a smell of starch and cleanliness. I took the tee-shirt and the pair of boxer shorts he handed me.

'I'll help you as much as I can. But you've got to promise to look after yourself. Come and give me that undertaker's bill when you're dressed.'

It was like stepping into a field of sweet grass that was filled with white daisies and butterflies silently flapping their wings in the sunshine.

'Christ, don't cry,' he said.

I dried my eyes in the bathroom. I put on lipstick and some kohl around my eyes. I looked better. I felt better. Claus had invited me to stay for the day. Perhaps it would be nice.

I got into the clothes he'd given me and then my green dress. At least I hadn't been sick on that. Then I turned to look at myself in the mirror. All things considered, I didn't look too bad.

*   *   *

I sat down beside Claus at the kitchen table and took the bill from Lambert's, which I had brought with me, out of my handbag. He looked at it for a moment, then went and fetched his cheque-book and wrote out the cheque, while on the other side of the table Johnnie watched him closely.

'There you are,' he said, tore the cheque out, and handed it to me. 'Oh no, change of plan,' he then continued. 'You let me keep this,' he said, taking back the cheque and picking up the bill, 'and I'll get my secretary to send them off tomorrow. You see, you get a complete service here,' he said, and walked through to the next room, to his desk, from where he got an envelope out of a drawer.

'You'll send me the other bills and things, won't you?' he called back.

'Yes,' I replied. I was rapturous. I was saved.

It was a lovely morning outside, a pale, clean, Sunday sky and not a cloud for miles.

Johnnie and I went through a gate in the speared railings and climbed to the top of Primrose Hill. London lay stretched below. We started trying to identify major buildings from the map on the steel plate in front of us.

Johnnie put an arm around my shoulder and pointed out St Paul's.

Oh yes. St Paul's, where Rudi and I had walked, one Sunday years before. St Paul's, where I'd taken the bloody photograph, the one I'd wept over in the chemist's. St Paul's. St Paul's.

I thought all this in one part of myself, but in another

I was registering pure, simple delight. I hadn't been touched by another human being for three months.

The next moment I looked at him. There was his big square body with its big square head resting on top. He had hung his jersey over his back and knotted it at the front.

We went down the hill again. In Prince Albert Road families were streaming towards the Zoo and the gutters were piled high with downy feathers. They came from the aviary nearby. The birds were moulting. The whole earth was stirring. I launched into my monologue, the one I'd delivered the night before. Summer made me feel happy but it also made me feel sad, et cetera. Johnnie received this in silence as we walked slowly together right across Regent's Park.

Near the mosque he bought me an ice-cream and tried to kiss me. I ran away from him laughing and he couldn't catch me.

I went home in the evening and I was happy. As soon as I got into bed Johnnie's face, with his green eyes and the gap between the two front teeth, floated up in my mind's eye. I tried to imagine what it would be like, making love to him, but I couldn't, and I fell asleep.

Twelve

39

My phone wasn't working (it wasn't cut off, just broken), and so I had arranged with Mr Sammi that I'd come in to work an hour later than usual. I popped in to Lambert's the undertakers to tell them a cheque was on the way.

'Had it in this morning,' said Mrs Lambert sourly after I had explained myself, and she picked up an envelope from her desk and waved it at me. It was Tuesday. That was quick, I thought. The envelope was addressed by hand with a fountain pen. The ink had smudged.

I went out into Goldhawk Road. A grimy, clapped-out London bus was coming along. Aimlessly, I hopped on, travelled as far as Queen Charlotte's Hospital and got out again. There was a flower stall outside the hospital gate. The vendor was sitting in a deck-chair reading a newspaper. He looked so spruce, he struck me as the sort of man who took a shower every day. He wore a thick gold bracelet on his wrist. Now that my troubles were over, I had set my mind on a big bunch of tulips, but I wanted red and he only had white. As I was dithering about, trying to decide whether to buy them or not, I saw another bus coming up the road. This one was going back in the direction of Shepherd's Bush.

I made it over in the nick of time. The conductor was a young man in a starched white shirt. When he helped me on, he squeezed my elbow. I went upstairs and sat down feeling relieved the bus had come and saved me from having to make a decision. I went to work.

My bills were paid. All of them.

Claus and Johnnie took to calling on Saturday morning. We would have breakfast in the Blue Sky and then go on to the Portobello Market. On Sundays we walked together on Hampstead Heath and in Richmond Park. Claus told stories and Johnnie paid court to me. I pretended to be unaware of his wooing while feeling secretly flattered, but was also strangely troubled by his desire. Sometimes I thought of Rudi.

•

Then I began to see him alone.

Then Johnnie invited me to a party at the Nine Lives. The gallery was five years old. I agreed.

He wrote my name in his pocket diary with a fountain pen and blew on the ink to make it dry.

The party was on a Thursday. When I got back from work I thought, I shan't make an effort. He can have me as I am. No make-up. Bare legs.

I went into the bedroom and looked at my face in the mirror.

Big wide forehead, I thought. I should be awfully

clever but I'm not. Brown eyes. Biggish nose – at least it doesn't try to pretend it's not there. Nice mouth but lips too thin. Where's the lipstick? . . .

In the taxi, Johnnie started to whistle. It wasn't a full-throated whistle with lips pursed but the other kind, through the teeth. The noise is high-pitched, like a piccolo.

I said, 'What's that?'

'Don't you recognize it?'

'"Lili Marlene?"'

'Why did you ask, then?'

'I speak before I think, I suppose,' I said.

Johnnie moved down the seat a few inches towards me.

'Look at the back of the cab-driver's neck,' he said.

It was thick and red and criss-crossed with lines. It was the kind of neck men had when I was a child.

'Do you see the great long scar there?'

I did. It was white and shiny, like the one on my knee.

'What's the first thing you can remember?' I asked.

'Everything before five is a bit of a blur, as far as I'm concerned, but I bet you remember everything. I bet you haven't forgotten anything.'

We passed the Royal Garden Hotel and then the very stretch where I had hurried in the mist towards Kensington Gardens in search of Claus. That all seemed very far away now, like something seen through a telescope held to the eye the wrong way. Then I wondered vaguely if I was still in love with Claus. Was that why I was here in a cab with the man who shared his house? I tried to follow this thought but it darted away, like a fish in the river at the approach of a shadow. It is easy to get confused when you think there's a choice.

The taxi pulled up outside the Nine Lives gallery. I got out nimbly and stood on the pavement with a broad smile. Johnnie paid and waited for his change.

Lo met us just inside the door. Short, shimmery dress through which her nipples showed faintly, and her long dark hair trailing over her shoulders.

Claus came up and said, 'Hello, dear.'

As he bent to kiss me, Lo was watching him.

'Did you get home all right the other day?' said Lo. She was addressing me. 'Not the other day. You know when I mean . . . whenever it was. Three weeks ago, four weeks ago, or something.'

Her Home Counties vowels were immaculate.

'Sorry?'

'Did you get home all right when we put you in the taxi?'

'Oh yes,' I said, suddenly grasping she was on about the afternoon I failed to notice that the wine in the bottles changed colour.

'Phew. That was lucky for you.' She rolled her eyes and then, turning to the men, she said, ''Cos have I got a story I could tell you about taxis.'

A rastafarian with a tray of tall glasses glided by.

I took one and drank. It was champagne. It prickled the back of my throat. Then I floated off from Claus and Lo and Johnnie. This was a mistake. I didn't know a soul and within seconds I had become the unattached leper you see at every party. I made a sterling effort not to let it look as if it mattered that no one was talking to

206

me and then I floated back to where I'd started. A group had now formed around Lo. I stood on the edge.

'So I got into the taxi and he drove off,' I heard Lo saying.

'I live in West London, in Hammersmith,' she said, 'but he set off over Battersea Bridge, heading south; "Excuse me", I said, "You're going the wrong way."

'"Don't worry, darling" he says' (Lo switched here to mock cockney). '"It may seem like a roundabout way to the west but it's quicker. Avoids the traffic."'

Claus was watching her with extraordinary attentiveness.

'All right, I thought.' She had switched back to Home Counties. 'But he keeps on going south. We go through Clapham and Streatham and finally Mitcham. I think, This is not a roundabout route. I'm being taken for a ride.'

'Oh, you poor thing,' said the woman standing next to me.

'So I say, "Will you please turn the taxi round."

'The driver says nothing. Just indicates and turns through a hole in a corrugated fence. I'm thinking, Oh Christ. I'm going to be murdered. I look out of the window. We're in the middle of a car-breaker's yard. Not a soul in sight.'

'He gets out of the driver's seat, comes round and opens the door. "Get out," he says. I think, He could be a killer. I'm just going to keep very calm, cool and collected, and I'm going to do exactly what he says.'

Everyone laughed.

'I get out. He has a big carrier bag with "Harrods" on it. He opens it. "Put everything in here," he says.'

Lo mimed the removal of her wristwatch and her

earrings. Claus was staring at her.

'So I put in my watch and my earrings and my handbag and he says, "Keep going." So I put in my shoes and my hairband and off come the trousers and the blouse. "Keep going," he says, and so in goes all my silk underwear. Then he gets in the taxi and drives away and I'm left standing there.'

'You mean, he left you with nothing?'

This was the woman beside me. She wore a fur hat and had piercing blue eyes.

'Absolutely,' said Lo theatrically, 'Nu-thing!'

'Fancy a taxi tonight?' Johnnie whispered in my ear.

I decided to take a look at the egg-shaped sculptures dotted on the podiums around the room.

The first piece was titled Mode 12, price £4,000; the second, Mode 13, price £4,500 (and amazingly it had sold); the third, Mode 14, price £3,750, and so on.

'Terrible, aren't they? All shit,' I heard a young man saying. I looked at him for a few moments before I realized from the long pony-tail and the mournful expression, that it was Freddie, the artist.

'Why do you say that?' I asked.

The tray floated past and I exchanged my empty glass for a new full one.

Claus was sitting on a chair now. For a moment, through a parting in the crowd, I glimpsed his hand on the back of Lo's smooth thigh. I was not surprised, but I was hurt. A moment later the crowd moved, and Claus and Lo were hidden again.

I said, 'You just take them for every penny they've got.'

I waggled my finger at everyone in the room.

'Every penny,' I repeated. 'They're rich. They won't mind. They want to give their money away.'

I winked at him slowly and squeezed his arm.

'Every penny.'

I had a recollection of Rudi. The day we married. Lifting my cross to admire it . . . and then looking at me as I lay back on the pillow.

40

We sat in the back of the second taxi of the evening. Johnnie took my hand in his. I squeezed back and he squeezed harder. I touched his shoulder with my cheek.

He took me to a bar in Mayfair with red velvet seats.

'What do you want to drink?' Johnnie asked. 'I'm going to have a vodka martini.'

'I'll go for that,' I said.

For want of anything better to say I said suddenly, 'I don't know what I'd do without Claus. He's saved my life.'

Johnnie looked at me from the other side of the table. Then he lifted his eyes and waggled a finger. The waitress came over. She had a sharp nose and was wearing very bright red lipstick. Her expression had something superior about it.

'Two vodka martinis.'

The waitress nodded and walked off and he looked at me again.

'I really don't know what I'd have done,' I said. 'If he hadn't come forward, my bacon would have been cooked.'

I expected some reaction, but instead he just rocked his big head backwards and forwards and then, appearing to be preoccupied by something, began listening as the man at the piano sang:

'Only the lone–ly . . .'

After listening for two or three minutes, Johnnie moved back a fraction in his seat. The waitress had appeared with the tray. She put two ice-cold glasses down on to the table and went off again.

'You know,' he began slowly, almost hesitantly, 'I think you should know I tore up Claus's cheque to the undertakers and paid it myself, and I've been paying ever since. I did this because I wanted to help you. I did this because I like you. Very much.' He wiped his mouth and continued, 'I feel a lot better now. I feel a weight's been taken off me. Well, that's that done,' he said and raised his glass. 'Your health.'

I lifted my glass, not sure what we were toasting.

'Cheers, then,' Johnnie said.

With my glass I touched Johnnie's, and then I put the rim to my lips and drank.

I said, 'You shouldn't have done that.'

At a fork in the road I thought I'd gone one way, but all along, and I didn't know it, I'd been redirected.

41

How do you explain these things?

You could say, 'I needed the money. I came home and went to bed with him.'

You could say, 'The flesh is weak. I came home and went to bed with him.'

You could say, 'I take comfort wherever I can. I came home and went to bed with him.'

That's all fine and dandy as far as it goes, but it's not the truth.

I went home with him, drunk. I undressed, drunk. I went to bed with him, drunk.

Now, that's a truth.

I don't know what you would call what happened next. He lifted his great heavy shape on to me and we moved together but the earth did not move.

We are neither of us sexual athletes. We are neither of us getting any younger. We're inept. We're hopeless. Yet we held each other as if this was the very last time. We were even tender.

That's another truth.

Life's a series of blows. What is it Rudi used to say? 'What is born a drum is beaten till death.'

Now, that's a truth.

My story on a postcard:

Once upon a time it was March and I was about to go to Brighton with my husband. He was what they call a petty crook. He wasn't anything of the sort to me but that's how he would be described by some. But now he is dead and gone and I am with Johnnie, the man I met the day Rudi died.

And now it is the end of summer and I am in a bedroom in Primrose Hill. Another man I loved is downstairs. He is the third man in all this. He is talking to my new lover. They own this house together.

I was lying here with Johnnie after our love-making when we heard, first the taxi pulling up outside and then the front door opening and banging shut as Claus came in.

'I'm going down to talk to him,' announced Johnnie, and he got up, pulled on a dressing-gown to cover his square, heavy body and went out.

And since he left I have been lying here and thinking, How did it happen.

One reason: I let him bludgeon me into it. I just let him wear my resistance down.

I know. That's the oldest excuse in the book.

Another reason: my first choice was lost to me.

Third reason: I wanted him.

Fourth reason: . . . It was summer. It was a summer in childhood. I had a white dress with blue polka dots

213

which tied at the back. The dots were the same colour as the sky which was the same colour as cornflowers.

Every morning when I woke up there was sunshine, bright behind our curtains, mixed with the smell of mown grass, and Mum's loaves cooling on the garden wall, and wood smoke from the fire in the kitchen.

I played all day in the garden or in the Dark House, or splashed around in the cold sea until my flesh stood up in goose pimples.

It was the time my dad was still at home and he used to bring us fudge on Saturdays, when he came home from work. It was soft, like putty, and I would put it against the roof of my mouth and press until it was moulded to the shape and then let it melt there.

My dress was the same colour as the sky was the same colour as cornflowers. It was the time my dad was still at home.

There was a pub in the countryside not far from where we lived. It was called the Drover's Arms. There was a picture of a shepherd holding a crook on the board outside. We used to go there.

One Sunday lunchtime we were sitting in the garden. There were daisies growing all over the lawn. I picked them by the dozen and carried them back to the table in the lap of my dress. With his penknife, my dad nicked slits in the green stems and joined them into a chain. It was a sturdy one, not like the kind Vicki and I made. Ours always fell apart in minutes.

He put it on my mum. She laughed and wriggled and blushed. Later, she took it off and went away to do something. My dad was talking to Vicki. I put the daisy chain over my head and ran off with it trailing over my shoulder.

In the corner of the garden there was a well. It was a brick well with a wooden gibbet. Just like a well in a fairy-tale. It was the custom to throw pennies and halfpennies in and to make wishes.

'Hey, look at me.' I called from the side of the well.

I took off the garland of daisies and held it over the side.

My dad called, 'Stop, don't do that. It's your mother's,' and I let it go and it fell slowly and it landed without a splash. I looked at it floating below; it was a perfect white circle on the dark waters.

'Why did you do that?' my mother asked, passing back from wherever she had been.

I told her. When I had let the daises go, I had made a wish. I had wished that my dad would not have to go to work, and could stay at home instead and play with Vicki and me. In my childish way, this is what I imagined he wanted.

Mum led me back by the hand to the table.

'You stupid brat,' my father said. 'Why did you do that? Why did you throw away that garland? Why would you throw away something which is beautiful?'

My face went red and my ears burned. I couldn't speak. I wanted to shout. I wanted to cry. My dad didn't love me any more. Then I heard my mum saying, 'It's not quite the way you think it is, Geoffrey,' and she explained the way I had made my wish for him before letting the garland slip from my fingers.

My dad called me to him and lifted me on to his lap. I put my head against his chest and he stroked my hair. He told me I was sweet. He told me he loved me. He told me he'd have given me a penny to throw in the well if I'd only asked. He told me we'd make another daisy chain and it didn't matter that the old one was gone.

He gave me sixpence. It was exquisite. Like food after hunger. Warmth after cold. Peace after argument.

The men's voices are louder downstairs. They are not arguing. It is simply that they have stood up and their heads are closer to the ceiling.

I can hear Johnnie's footsteps now. He is slowly climbing the long, wide stairs.

The garland and the wishing well. It's my favourite story about myself. I haven't told it yet to Johnnie, but then we've only just begun.

He has gone into the lavatory. Just a pee and a flush and then he will be in here.

I've made my bed, as my mother would say, and now I'm going to lie in it.

MALACHY AND HIS FAMILY

Carlo Gébler

'I THINK ALL THE BAD WHICH HAS HAPPENED STAYS IN THE BLOOD'

The blood of Malachy's family is a strange mixture. Malachy is not – as he had thought for 25 years – the son of the stockbroker who commutes daily to New York. His real father is an Irishman who now lives in a prosperous London suburb with his Hungarian-exile wife, their daughter Eva and their son – also called Malachy.

On his first visit to them in England, Malachy starts a notebook, prompted by too much amphetamine taken one night with his half-siblings. In it he records everything he does, sees and feels – revealing his developing fascination and passion for his half-sister; uncovering the things that fester in a family's blood.

'A truly international story of genealogy, immigration and emigration, following routes through the twentieth century to New Jersey, Ireland, Eastern Europe, Northampton and the suburbs of Surrey . . . With so much resonant material in the book, it's hard not to agree with Malachy when he says "a story remains in the mind when everything else goes"'
Irish Times

'Ingenuity abounds . . . Gébler brings to life the idea that we are not only shaped by our experiences and by genetics but also by the bad experiences of our forebears . . . Gébler is a writer of tremendous ability'
Time Out

'Zips along effortlessly: his ability to zoom in on telling, occasionally riveting external illustrations of mood and character is almost unique on this side of the Atlantic'
Daily Telegraph

'An intriguing and highly effective novel'
Today

0 349 10194 9
FICTION

If Samuel Beckett had been born in Czechoslovakia we'd still be waiting for Godot.

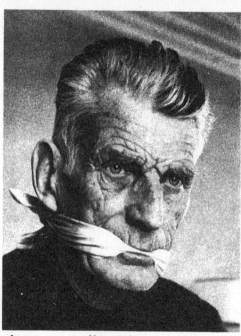

Samuel Beckett's "Waiting for Godot" is banned in Czechoslovakia.

In fact, any writing that differs from the opinions of the Czech government is banned in Czechoslovakia.

Luckily, Beckett does not live in Czechoslovakia, but what of those writers who do?

Fortunately, some of their work can be read in Index on Censorship, a magazine which fights censorship by publishing the work of censored poets, authors, playwrights, journalists and publishers.

We publish work from all over the world regardless of politics, religion or race.

Our contributions come from wherever work is censored.

We also publish commentaries, first-hand testimonials, factual reports and a country by country chronicle.

You'll always find publishers, writers and journalists at the front of the struggle for free speech.

Now you know where you can find their work.

Please write to us for a free copy of our magazine at: 39c Highbury Place, London N5 1QP or you can telephone us on: 01-359 0161.

Index on Censorship for crying out loud.